R.L. STINE

FEAR STREET®

HALLOWEEN PARTY

Mahmood Imam

Simon Pulse

New York London Toronto Sydney

A Parachute Press book

SIMON PULSE
An imprint of Simon & Schuster Children's Publishing Division
1230 Avenue of the Americas, New York, NY 10020
Copyright © 1990 by Parachute Press, L.L.C.
All rights reserved, including the right of reproduction in
whole or in part in any form.
SIMON PULSE and colophon are registered trademarks
of Simon & Schuster, Inc.
FEAR STREET is a registered trademark of Parachute Press, Inc.
Designed by Sammy Yuen Jr.
The text of this book was set in Times.
Manufactured in the United States of America
First Simon Pulse edition August 2006
10 9 8 7 6 5
Library of Congress Control Number 2005933855
ISBN-13: 978-1-4169-1811-0
ISBN-10: 1-4169-1811-6

HALLOWEEN PARTY

the <u>best</u> halloween costumes

- Edward Scissorhands
- Anything from The Twilight Zone
- Beetlejuice
- Anyone from a Tim Burton character

chapter

1

*T*he tombstone loomed gray in the moonlight, its edges eroded into irregular shapes. Thick moss covered the words etched into its surface, except for a line at the bottom.

DIED OCTOBER 31, 1884

Terry Ryan tried to step quickly past the ancient monument, but his girlfriend, Niki Meyer, pulled on his hand to stop him. "Look, Terry," she said. "The person in this grave died on this same day over a hundred years ago."

Niki stepped closer, her flashlight casting a dim yellow arc of light on the gravestone. Terry pulled his jacket tighter. The wind howled, sounding like the wail of a creature long dead. Somewhere something scratched and rattled against stone.

I don't believe I'm standing in the middle of the Fear Street Cemetery at night, Terry thought. He took Niki's hand again and gave it a gentle squeeze. She turned to him, her beautiful dark eyes bright with excitement. In her red gown and black cape she looked like a medieval princess.

"I wonder who all these people were," she said, gesturing at the crumbling gravestones.

"Early settlers of Shadyside, probably," said Terry. "Nobody's been buried here for years."

"It's spooky here," Niki said. "But kind of beautiful too. How do you suppose all those stories got started, about the living dead coming out of their graves?"

"Just stories," he said. "Come on. Let's go."

The wind gusted, and Terry saw Niki shiver inside her cape. They began walking again, and Terry picked a path through the weed-choked lanes between the grave markers. With their every step, the ground creaked, a sound like breaking bones. Somewhere above them the wind shrieked, tearing at a branch. Terry stole a glance at Niki. Her eyes were sparkling with excitement.

The howling wind doesn't bother Niki, Terry thought. Niki had been nearly deaf since an accident in second grade. But she spoke so clearly and read lips so well, most people didn't even realize she couldn't hear.

Niki herself never acted as if she was different from other kids. She never wanted special treatment at all. In fact—just the opposite. Niki was always ready for adventure.

But was she ready for tonight?

They were almost at the end of the shortcut that led to the edge of the graveyard. Beyond the cemetery's stone wall Terry could see the outline of the old Cameron mansion. The tall trees around it were whipping from side to side. From this distance it looked as if the house were slowly shaking itself.

The wooden gate at the edge of the wall hung open. Without realizing it, Terry began to walk a little faster. Niki tugged on his hand again. "I dropped my mask back there," she said. "It'll just take a second to get it."

Holding the flashlight on her feet, Niki quickly retraced her steps. "Not so fast," Terry called, then he remembered she couldn't hear him. She ducked behind the tombstone she'd been examining. "I've got it!" she called.

Terry slipped on a moss-covered rock, then quickly pulled himself up and headed to the tombstone. Even if the scary stories weren't true, he didn't want to let Niki out of his sight. He had almost reached the tombstone when a sudden high-pitched scream split the air.

"Niki!" he called. His heart thudding, he lunged behind the tombstone. Niki was there, brushing the dirt off her black silk mask. "What's wrong?" she asked when she saw his face.

"I heard a—" The scream was repeated. "There it is again!" he said. He put his arm around Niki and held her tight.

The sound had come from the direction of the gate. He thought of going back the way they had come and walking *around* the cemetery. But it would take too long. Besides, he wanted to get out of the graveyard as soon as possible.

With the flashlight in one hand and his other arm around Niki, Terry walked cautiously toward the gate.

They had nearly reached it when a tall, dark figure suddenly jumped into the path in front of them.

Niki let out a shriek and pressed tighter against Terry.

Blocking the path was a figure from a nightmare. The thing's black clothing hung in tatters. Its face—or what was left of it—seemed to be rotting away. And the flesh on its hands was peeling off the bones.

This isn't happening, Terry thought. That thing can't be real.

His hands shaking, he pushed Niki behind him and raised the flashlight threateningly. Can a weapon hurt the living dead? he wondered.

But before he could find out, the figure suddenly reached up and ripped its head off, revealing the grinning face of Murphy Carter. It took Terry a moment to realize that the gruesome head was only a mask.

"Gotcha!" Murphy said. "Boy, you two were scared to death! You should have seen your faces."

"Yeah, sure," said Terry, hoping his voice wasn't shaking. "We knew it was you all along."

"Sure you did," said Murphy. "And my grandmother's the mayor of Shadyside." He grinned at Niki, then gestured with one of the gloves that looked like a rotting hand. "Come on, let's go," he said. "We wouldn't want to be late for *this* party."

chapter
2

Two Weeks Earlier

*S*ometimes Terry thought he tried to do too many things. Sometimes he knew he did. That week alone, in addition to his regular schoolwork and after-school job, he had to turn in a science project and chair a student council meeting. He also promised his little sister he'd help her learn to ride her new bicycle.

His head was so full of his projects, he had to twirl the combination on his locker twice before he could get it to open. And after he did, he realized he'd been meaning to clean out his locker.

It was hard to believe so much junk could fit inside such a small space. Carefully Terry began to push aside his jacket, his tennis racket, half a dozen books, and the props for his science project. "It's here somewhere," he told himself. "I know it is."

"What's somewhere?" asked a voice behind him. Terry turned, startled, to see Trisha McCormick standing behind him. Trisha was a short brunette with wiry hair. She was also the most friendly and enthusiastic person Terry knew.

"Hi, Trisha," he said. "What did you say?"

"Who were you talking to?" asked Trisha.

"Uh—myself," said Terry. "I'm a real good listener."

"Sorry," said Trisha, giggling. "I didn't mean to eavesdrop."

"I was looking for my lunch," Terry explained. "Aha.! There it is!" Triumphantly he pulled the rumpled brown bag from the jumble, noting with dismay that one whole side of it was wet. Shoving the rest of the stuff back in his locker, he slammed the door. As he did, a piece of paper fluttered to the floor.

"What's that?" said Trisha.

"I don't know," said Terry. He picked it up and examined it. It was a plain white envelope with a black border. On the front, in ornate lettering, was his name: Terry Ryan.

"Would you hold my lunch?" he asked Trisha. Curious, he opened the envelope. Inside was a stiff white card with a picture of a coffin on it. Beneath the coffin was written, "Reserved for YOU."

"A coffin?" Terry said, starting to laugh. "What is this—an ad for a funeral parlor?"

"Turn it over," Trisha said.

Terry did as she suggested. The other side was filled with writing. "Hey," he said.

"It's an invitation to a Halloween party at Justine Cameron's place, right?" said Trisha.

"Yeah," said Terry. "How did you know?"

"I got one too," said Trisha. "Probably everyone in

school did. But read what the invitation says. It's really weird."

"'All-Night Halloween Costume Party,'" Terry read. "All night. Hey, that's cool! Where's the weird part?"

"Keep going," said Trisha.

"'Special surprises,'" Terry read. "'Dancing, games.' I don't see what's so—"

"Did you read *where* it is?" said Trisha.

"'Cameron mansion, eight P.M. Friday night, October thirty-first,'" Terry read. "So?"

"So that's the old Cameron mansion," said Trisha. "The one that's out behind the cemetery on Fear Street."

"You're kidding! How can anyone have a party there? No one's lived in that place for years," said Terry.

"Justine and her uncle live there now," said Trisha. "They're fixing it up. I know because my father's firm is doing the electrical work."

"Wasn't that house supposed to be haunted?" Terry asked.

"Everything on Fear Street is supposed to be haunted," said Trisha. "Here's your squashed lunch back."

"Thanks," said Terry. As he and Trisha walked to the lunchroom, he thought about some of the things he'd heard about Fear Street. Although perfectly ordinary people lived in some of its beautiful old houses, other homes were deserted and rumored to harbor evil spirits. Terrible things had happened on Fear Street—murders, mysterious disappearances. It seemed like the perfect spot for a Halloween party.

"Why do you suppose Justine invited us to her party?" Trisha asked Terry at the cafeteria door.

Terry shrugged. "Beats me," he said. "I don't even know her. I just know what she looks like."

Everyone in the school knew what Justine looked like, Terry thought. She was the most beautiful girl at Shadyside High—maybe in the whole town. Even the girls thought so. She was tall and slim, and looked more like a model than a student, with her long shiny blond hair and eyes as green as jade. Justine was a transfer student, new to Shadyside High, and so far, hardly anyone had gotten to know her—though most of the boys had tried.

Terry was about to ask Trisha more about Justine when he spotted Niki sitting at a table by the door. He excused himself and slid in across from Niki so she'd be able to read his lips. "Hi, Funny Face," he said, calling her by his special pet name.

"Hi, Terry," Niki said, giving him a big smile. Terry suddenly felt like the most important person in the world. Niki always had that effect on him. He'd been going with her six months now, and he still couldn't believe his good fortune. Niki wasn't the prettiest girl at Shadyside, or the smartest, but she was definitely the most special.

When she came into a room, everybody automatically felt happier. When Niki smiled, her even white teeth flashing against her smooth olive skin, it was like the sun coming up.

"Whatcha been up to?" Niki asked him.

"Nothing much," Terry said. "But look at this." He handed her the invitation.

"I got one too," said Niki.

"Maybe everyone in the school did," said Terry.

"I don't think so," said Niki. "No one else in my homeroom got one. And none of my friends, like Jade and Deena, were invited."

"I wonder why she invited *us*," said Terry. "I don't even know her. Do you?"

"Not very well," Niki admitted. "She's in my gym class and I've played basketball with her. But we've hardly spoken to each other."

Terry opened his lunch, noting that the leak was coming from his meat loaf and tomato sandwich, which had somehow gotten completely smashed. "Ugh," he said, looking at the gooey mess.

"Here, have half of mine," said Niki. She always ate the same thing—a peanut butter and banana sandwich with celery and carrot sticks on the side.

"That's okay," said Terry. "Maybe I'll get chips from the vending machine."

"I can't believe the junk you eat," said Niki. "At least have some carrot sticks."

Terry took one and began to munch.

"What are you going to go as?" asked Niki.

"What?"

"To Justine's party. It's a costume party, remember?"

"Oh, I don't know," said Terry. "Maybe we ought to just skip it. None of your friends are going. And we don't really know Justine. . . ."

"So what?" said Niki. "I love costume parties. Besides, I've never been to a party on Fear Street".

"It would definitely be a first," said Terry.

"So it's settled," said Niki. "Besides, I'd like to get to know Justine better."

"What's she like in gym?" Terry asked.

"She's the best athlete in the class," said Niki. "She's in really great shape. I asked her about it once, and she told me she lifts weights."

Terry let out a low whistle. "Whoa!" he said. "No wonder she's so . . ." He let the thought trail off.

"She's so *what?*" asked Niki. She had a dangerous glint in her eyes.

"So—*you* know," he said, stifling a grin. He looked closely at Niki to see if she was really upset or was just teasing him.

"So—*stacked?*" Niki suggested.

"Well, yeah," said Terry.

Niki burst out laughing. "You boys are all alike!" she said. "I wonder who Justine asked to the party as her date."

For the rest of the day no one talked about anything but Justine and her party. Everyone had heard about it, even though not that many people had been invited.

Just before the bell rang for the last period, Lisa Blume stopped Terry in the hall. Lisa was assistant editor of the school paper, and she usually knew everything that was going on. In fact, she was a real gossip, except she called it being a reporter.

"I hear you were invited to Justine's party," she said to Terry. "Why do you think she asked you?"

"I don't have any idea," said Terry. "You're the reporter—maybe you can tell me."

"My theory is she wants to get to know people better," said Lisa. "But she's shy about it because of all the awful stories about the house where she lives."

"What are you talking about?"

"Don't you know?" said Lisa. "The last owners of the Cameron mansion were killed in some kind of accident years ago. The story is that no one could ever live there again because their spirits haunt the place."

"Nice story. So why is Justine living there?" asked Terry skeptically.

Lisa shrugged. "According to my aunt, Justine is a distant cousin of the original owners. Her uncle inherited the place and decided to fix it up."

"I heard she lives there with her uncle."

"He's her guardian," said Lisa. "I guess her parents an dead or divorced or something. Supposedly, Justine and her uncle have lived all over the country and even in Europe."

Terry knew that Lisa's information was usually right, but he didn't see what Justine had to do with him and Niki. He was still puzzling the matter over in biology class when Ricky Schorr sat down next to him.

Ricky was an obnoxious practical joker, and some people considered him the biggest nerd in the whole school. Ricky's thick black hair was uncombed as usual, and as usual he was wearing a tacky T-shirt no one else would be caught dead in. This one was stained with orange juice and said "Kiss Me, I'm a Martian."

"Hey, Schorr," said Terry.

"Yo, Terry," said Ricky. He set a rumpled paper sack down on the lab table separating them. "I heard you and Niki got invited to Justine's party."

"That's right," said Terry.

"So did I," said Ricky.

"Huh? No bull?" Terry was surprised. He couldn't imagine why Justine had chosen him and Niki, but it was even weirder that she had asked Ricky and Trisha. None of them hung out together.

"I wonder who else is going," Ricky said. "Have you heard?"

"Nope," said Terry. "How's your biology project coming?" he asked, deliberately changing the subject.

"I'm just about done," said Ricky. "In fact, I've got it in here." He pointed to the paper sack.

Terry looked at the sack in disbelief. It was throbbing and beginning to inch across the lab table. "I hate to tell you," he said, "but your science project seems to be trying to escape."

Ricky opened the sack. Instantly a small green frog leapt out and began hopping along the table. Terry grabbed for it and held it distastefully in his hands. "This is your biology project, Schorr?" he said. "A frog?"

"It's not the whole thing," said Ricky, looking hurt. He reached in the bag and pulled out a jar of murky water. "My project is on metamorphosis," he said. "I've got tadpoles in here."

Terry gazed at the jar doubtfully. "You mean you *had* tadpoles," he said. "Those aren't moving."

"Let me see," said Ricky. He took the jar and studied it closely, turning it first one way and then another. Then he shook it. "I guess I should have cut air holes in the lid," he said finally. "Oh, well, that's life, huh? Here today, slimy and disgusting tomorrow. I can always pick up some more at the pond." Terry handed him the frog, and he shoved it and the jar of dead tadpoles back into the sack.

"Great project, Schorr," Terry said sarcastically.

"Just call me Mr. Wizard," Ricky said.

"So who else is invited to the party?" Ricky asked after a moment.

"I don't know," said Terry. "Trisha McCormick. I don't know anyone else."

"Murphy Carter," said Ricky.

Murphy Carter was the first name on the list that made sense to Terry. Murphy was a linebacker on the football team and was known as an all-around party guy. But he had nothing in common with the rest of them.

Terry was about to ask Ricky more when Mr. Rothrock came in, ready to talk about genetics, and for the next forty minutes Terry forgot all about the party. But after school, walking outside to meet Niki, he passed a crowd gathered on the front steps. Lisa Blume was talking to a small crowd of students. Niki caught up with him on the sidewalk and took his elbow.

"Hi, Terry," she said. "How was your day?"

"Weird," said Terry honestly. "How about you?"

"Pretty weird too. I feel like a celebrity because of the invitation to the party."

"Which way do you want to walk home?" Terry asked.

"I guess by the— Wait a minute," said Niki. "Lisa's reading off a list." She squinted to where Lisa was speaking. Maybe to make up for her deafness, Niki's eyesight was great, and she could read lips across a room. "She's figured out everyone who's invited to the party," Niki said. "It's nine people. . . ."

"Only *nine?*" said Terry.

"That's what she says. There's you and me, Trisha, Ricky Schorr, Murphy Carter, Angela Martiner, Les Whittle, David Sommers, and—and Alex Beale."

"Alex? Oh, wonderful," Terry muttered sarcastically. For years he and Alex had been best friends. They had grown up together, played tennis together, even gone out with girls together—until last year when Niki had stopped going with Alex and started dating Terry. Alex had never gotten over his feelings for Niki—and sometimes Terry wondered if Niki was over *her* feelings for Alex.

"This whole list is bizarro," Niki was saying. "None of us hang out together, except maybe Murphy and David." David, like Murphy, was on the football team and also played basketball. Angela was a slim, pretty redhead with a fast reputation, and Les was a science whiz who kept to himself. Terry couldn't think why any of them had been invited.

But if Alex Beale was on the list, he was suddenly glad that he was too.

"Oh, look," said Niki. "Here comes Justine. Maybe she'll explain the list."

Justine came walking briskly out the front door of the school. As she did, the crowd moved closer to her. Reluctantly Terry followed Niki up on the steps.

"Where have you been all day?" someone asked Justine.

"I had a doctor's appointment in Waynesbridge," said Justine. "I just got back for last period."

"Come on," said Lisa. "Explain your guest list."

"What's to explain?" said Justine sweetly. "I'm just having a party."

"I've got it!" said Murphy Carter. "If you look at

the list, everyone invited is either a jock or a wimp, or someone's girlfriend. Is that it, Justine?"

"I'm sorry. I don't know what you're talking about," she said with a shrug. "I just invited some people I want to get to know better." She was wearing a body-hugging white wool dress, and with her frosty blond hair and green eyes she looked more like a model than ever.

"I like Murphy's idea," said David. "The wimps and the jocks."

"So what do you think, *wimp?*" asked Murphy, spotting Terry. "You got the guts to go to the party—and stay all night?"

"I hope you'll *all* come to the party," said Justine. She turned her dazzling smile on Murphy. "Can I count on you, Murphy?" she said.

"Uh—sure," he said, suddenly looking goofy.

"You can count on me too," said David.

"I'm glad," said Justine. "Now, both of you have to promise that you'll dance with me. I have a really *sweet* sound system, and I bought a lot of *excellent* dance CDs."

Justine was laying it on pretty thick, and Terry could see that Murphy and David were buying it.

"Hey, I'd like to dance with you," said Bobby McCorey, who had appeared from somewhere with his buddy, Marty Danforth. Bobby was on the varsity football team, but he had a bad temper and most of the other guys didn't hang out with him. He and Marty were the biggest bullies in the school.

"Well, I'd like to dance with you too, Bobby," said Justine, her voice suddenly sarcastic. "Why don't you come to my aerobics class?"

The other kids laughed, and Bobby glared at them before turning back to Justine. "Why don't I come to your party instead?" he said. "You probably just forgot to send me an invitation, right?"

"No," said Justine, smiling again. "I didn't forget."

"Well, you'd better change your mind," said Bobby with a scowl. "Me and Marty don't like to be left out of things."

"I'm sorry you feel that way," said Justine. "But this is a small party, and you guys just aren't on the list."

"We'll see about that!" said Bobby menacingly. "Come on, Marty," he added. "Let's leave these dorks and go have some fun." He and Marty stalked away, then jumped on their motorcycles and roared off. Terry had a feeling they weren't giving up, but Justine didn't seem at all concerned.

"Hey, Justine—what about dates?" Murphy asked. "I can bring my girlfriend, can't I?"

"It's not a party for dates," said Justine. "It's not that kind of party at all."

"But Monica and I have been going together for two years," said Murphy.

"Then I'm sure she won't mind giving you a little space for just one night," said Justine.

Terry and Niki were turning to leave when the front door to the school swung open with a bang. Alex Beale came swaggering down the steps, his huge, muscular frame seeming to take up all the space a foot around him. Terry had to admit that Alex was good-looking, with his short blond hair, his confident smile, his laughing, dark eyes. As soon as he got close to Justine, he winked.

"Got your invitation," he said.

"Good," said Justine. "I hope I can count on you."

"Oh, you can count on me," said Alex. "One, two, three, four, five . . ."

What comes after five, Alex? Terry thought. The sight of Alex always made Terry feel uneasy and sarcastic these days.

"I knew I could count on you, Alex," Justine said, smiling again. She turned and gave a little wave to the kids who were still there. "See the rest of you later," she said, and strolled out to the parking lot.

Terry took Niki's hand and tugged gently. But before they could get down the steps, Murphy Carter's voice cut through the noise. "Hey, Terry," he said. *"Wimp.* Where you going so fast?"

"We're going home," said Terry. "What do you think?"

"Right," said Murphy. "But you never answered my question." Quickly he explained to Alex about the invitations going either to wimps or jocks. "So I asked Terry if he thought he could go the distance and stay all night."

"Good question," said Alex, laughing. "Can *you?"*

"Oh, wow. A haunted house," said Terry. "I'm shaking in my shoes."

Alex used his best Count Dracula voice to say: "Even if it's on Fear Street?"

"It's just another street, as far as I'm concerned," said Murphy. "All that garbage about evil things happening there is just superstition."

"I'm not so sure about that," said Alex thoughtfully.

"Now who's the wimp?" cracked Murphy, slightly confused. "Hey, Alex, whose side are you on?"

"Give me a break, Murphy," Alex said, rolling his

17

dark eyes. "Halloween on Fear Street? I'm ready." He turned back to Terry, an odd smirk on his handsome face. "What about it, Terry? Think you and the wimps'll be able to stay all night in a haunted house?"

"I've got no problem with it," said Terry. "But are you sure your mommy will let you stay out after dark?"

Alex ignored Terry's shot and called to Ricky Schorr, who was headed to the parking lot, carrying the paper bag with his dead biology project. "Hey, Schorr!" he shouted. "How about you? You going to join Terry's team and show up at the party?"

"Sure I'll show up," said Ricky. "And I'm not a wimp."

Alex, David, and Murphy laughed. "I love it!" said Murphy. "He's not a wimp!"

"He doesn't have the *guts* to be a wimp!" cried David.

The three of them started laughing all over again, slapping one another high-fives.

"So who else is on your 'team,' Terry?" asked Alex. "Les Whittle, maybe—and Trisha? Think they'll have the guts to go?"

"Ask them yourself," said Terry. He took a deep breath.

Niki gave him a worried look, then turned to the jocks. "Come on, guys," she said. "This isn't a contest —it's a party. Why can't we all just—"

"Sorry, Niki," said Murphy. "Maybe it started out as a party, but it's a contest now. Us against them. The jocks—against the wimps."

Terry stood there a moment, exasperated. Alex was always trying to show him up. Why couldn't he just accept that Niki was his girlfriend now?

"Find someone else to play your games," he said finally. "Come on, Niki."

"In other words," said Alex, "you're too chicken to go. In that case, Niki, maybe you'd better join our team. Sounds like Terry's not sure he can protect you."

"I can take care of Niki—obviously better than you!" Terry shouted, losing his temper and immediately feeling embarrassed about it.

"Will you both stop acting like children!" Niki shouted. "I can take care of myself! And for your information I'm not on any so-called team! That's the dumbest idea I've ever heard!"

"Oh, yeah?" said Alex, looking stung. "Maybe you ought to think twice about that." He took a step forward, his face suddenly dark with anger.

"Take it easy, Alex," Terry said. "Nobody meant anything. It's just a party, all right?"

"It's more than that now," muttered Alex. "And you know it." He turned and walked quickly to the parking lot.

The crowd of kids began to break up. "Yo—Captain Wimp," Ricky cheerfully called from across the parking lot. "We're going to cream those guys, huh, dude?"

"They don't have a chance," Terry called back, suddenly into the competition without realizing it. "We'll show them who the real wimps are. And it's not us."

He started to reach for Niki's hand, but stopped in surprise. She was standing still and staring up at him, her face full of misery. "Hey, Funny Face," he said. "What's the matter?"

"This stupid contest," she said, frowning. "Why'd you let those guys push you into it?"

"Nobody pushed me into anything," said Terry. "Besides, it's nothing to worry about. It's just a goof."

"To you, maybe," Niki said. "But not to Alex. Didn't you see his face? He's serious about this! Deadly serious."

chapter

3

Terry's parents readily agreed to let him go to the all-night party, but only because Justine's uncle was going to chaperon. Niki's parents were harder to persuade, but when Niki showed them the costume she'd spent hours making, they finally gave in.

Meanwhile, Terry, Ricky, Les, and Trish—the "wimp" team—were thinking up tricks to play on the jocks. Terry only joined in halfheartedly, knowing that the real competition was between Alex and him.

Niki absolutely refused to have anything to do with any competition or pranks. But she was really looking forward to the party.

Meanwhile, every day at school was like April Fool's Day. At first it was just harmless fun.

One morning the jocks "punk'd" Ricky Schorr with a huge plastic snake that jumped out of his locker.

Then Les got even by sneaking into the locker room

and filling Alex's and Murphy's basketball shoes with shaving cream.

The day after that, Trisha received a phone call from someone who told her she had won a thousand pounds of dead fish in a wimp contest.

But then the pranks turned ugly. Two days before Halloween Terry opened his locker and reached for his tennis racket without looking.

"Ohhh."

Something in there brushed against his hand.

It felt clammy and cold. Like dead flesh.

Terry dropped the racket in disgust.

He took a step back, then forced himself to look down at the racket.

Hanging from the strings, a plucked chicken head was staring up at him through sightless eyes.

"Oh, gross."

He picked up the racket and unwrapped the note taped around the handle: "Here's a start on your costume, wimp. You'll see worse—unless you chicken out and forget the party."

"Very mature, Alex," Terry said to the empty hall.

He shrugged, then threw the chicken head and note into the nearest trash can. How could he and Alex have become such enemies? he wondered. He could remember the years growing up, when Alex's family had lived just down the street.

They had been such good friends then. Inseparable, almost.

Now they couldn't be together for five minutes without getting into some dumb competition.

It was dumb, so dumb.

But even though he knew it was dumb, Terry still didn't want to lose to Alex. Not now. Not ever.

On Thursday before the party Terry was hurrying to the school library to do some work on his biology project during study period. He'd chosen seed germination for his project because it seemed really interesting. It *was* really interesting, but it was also a lot more complicated than he had ever imagined.

He had tried to germinate some seeds and preserve them in different stages of growth, but nothing would sprout. He was going to have to draw illustrations instead.

He rounded the corner just before the library and stopped dead. At the end of the hall was a small group of kids, including Murphy, David, Alex—and Niki. Niki was wearing a bright red sweater and a plaid skirt, and looked so pretty all he wanted to do was go up and hug her. But she was smiling and talking with Alex.

Alex spotted Terry first. He didn't say anything. He just stared at Terry as if he were a bug or some other low form of life. And then he deliberately refocused on Niki. He bent forward and said something to her, very close to her face. Niki shook her head quickly, looking annoyed, and the jocks laughed and swaggered off. Terry forced himself to act as if he hadn't noticed anything. "Hi, Funny Face," he said.

"Hi, Terry," said Niki. She smiled, but it wasn't her full smile. She seemed worried, as if something was on her mind.

"What was that all about?" he said casually.

"What was what all about?"

"With Murphy and Alex. What were you talking about?"

For a moment Niki didn't answer, then she gave Terry the Look, the look that meant he was on dangerous ground. "Why shouldn't I talk to them?" she asked, sounding defensive.

"Well, it's just that—that they're on the other team," said Terry. Then, trying to make a joke out of it, he added, "After all, this is war!"

But Niki didn't take it as a joke. "For your information," she said, "it's no such thing. And I'm not on either team. Or had you forgotten?"

"I remembered, but—well, you're going to the party with *me*, so . . ."

"I'll go to the party with you," Niki said. "But I'll talk to anyone I want."

Terry knew she was right. "I'm sorry," he said. "Didn't mean to come on so heavy. It's just that you look sort of worried."

"As a matter of fact, I *am* worried," said Niki. "This whole party is beginning to seem weirder and weirder."

"What do you mean?"

"Well, this dumb contest. Justine is really into it too. And I still can't figure out the guest list. This group just doesn't belong together."

"I know," said Terry. "But so what?"

"And why did she say no one could bring dates?" Niki went on.

"That's not a problem for *us*," said Terry. "Are you saying you don't want to go?"

"No," said Niki. "But, Terry, be careful. This morning Angela told me the jocks are cooking up some tricks for the party that could be really dangerous."

"Like what?"

"I don't know. That's what I was asking Alex about."

"What did he say?"

"He wouldn't tell me. He just said I should join his team," Niki replied, even more upset now. "He said it might not be safe for me to go with the wimps!"

Terry took a deep breath and held it. "What did you tell him?" he asked for a moment. He hated himself for asking, but he had to know.

"Oh, I said he was right and I'd decided to go with the jocks—what do you think?"

The sarcasm in her voice was as heavy as cement, and Terry felt terrible. "Niki, I'm sorry. I didn't mean—"

"What good does it do to be sorry?" she said. "I can't believe the way you and Alex are acting. You're both taking this whole thing so seriously! Why can't you lighten up and just see it as a party?"

"Hey, it's not me who's taking it too seriously," Terry said. "Alex is the one who's playing tricks. He's the one who's threatening you, trying to cause trouble between us—"

"Will you listen to yourself?" said Niki, her dark eyes suddenly flashing in anger. "Why don't you just admit that you're as jealous of Alex as he is of you! That's what's really behind this stupid competition!"

She turned angrily and walked down the hall.

Terry thought of going after her, but stopped himself. It wouldn't do any good. When Niki got that mad, it always took her a while to cool off.

Terry had the library all to himself during study period, but he might as well have been in the middle of a crowded train station for all the work he got done on his project. He stared at photographs of seeds, but all he could see was the face of Alex Beale.

Whatever Alex was up to, he thought, he wasn't

going to get away with it. And Terry refused to be scared off by talk of "dangerous" tricks. After all, it was just a Halloween party. He expected a few scares on Halloween—trick or treat, and all that.

But as much as he tried to make light of it, Terry couldn't ignore a tiny shiver of foreboding.

Terry was on his way from the library to his next class when he heard angry voices just outside the delivery entrance to the cafeteria. He was about to go on by when he heard a small scream and the frightened voice of a girl: "Stop it! You're hurting me!"

His heart thudding, Terry pulled the door all the way open. Standing on the service porch were Bobby McCorey and Marty Danforth. Between them was Justine, her face pale and her expression frightened.

"I can't!" Justine was saying. "Don't you understand? The party is already set—"

"Well, you'd better un-set it," said Bobby, sounding really tough.

Justine tried to get away, but Marty had hold of her wrist.

"Like we told you, Justine," he said. "We don't take no for an answer."

Terry walked up to them without even thinking. "All right, you two," he said. "Let her go."

"Oh, yeah?" said Bobby. "Who says so?"

"I do," said Terry. "Come on."

"You don't scare me," said Bobby. But he did let go of Justine's wrist.

"Come on, Bobby," said Marty. "We can finish this later."

"And don't think we won't," added Bobby. He started to go inside, but stopped suddenly and turned to glare at Justine. "You've got till tomorrow night to change your mind," he told her.

"Forget it," said Justine. "You're not coming."

"We'll see about that," sneered Marty. "And as for you, *wimp*," he added, pointing at Terry, "if you don't stay out of my face, you won't need a Halloween mask."

Swaggering, the two bullies disappeared into the hall.

Justine stared after them a moment. "Nice guys," she said.

"They think they're so tough," Terry said. "When it comes down to it, they're probably the two biggest cowards in Shadyside."

"Well, I think what you did was really brave," Justine said, giving him a brilliant and somehow intimate smile. "Thank you."

Terry noticed that she had her shiny blond hair pulled back in a braid and was wearing a lime-colored sweater that made her green eyes appear even greener.

"Hey, listen, don't worry about those two," said Terry. Then suddenly he realized what he'd done. He'd stood up to the two meanest guys at Shadyside.

I could've been *dead meat!* he thought.

Was I out of my head, or what?

"You were wonderful," Justine said. "Some day I'd like to show you just how grateful I am." She let her smile linger, then went on. "I also want to apologize to you," she added, her musical voice low and intimate.

"Apologizer?" said Terry, surprised. "For what?"

Justine looked embarrassed. "I—I understand that my party invitations have caused some trouble. That there's some sort of contest."

"Well, yeah," said Terry. "But it's not your fault."

"Thank you for saying so," said Justine. "I never meant the party to cause any bad feelings. All I really want to do is have a few special people over so I can get to know you all better." For a moment she lightly rested her fingertips on Terry's arm. He felt a jolt of electricity travel up his arm and then through his body.

"Well—uh—hey, I mean— We'd, uh—we'd all like to get to know you better too," he stammered.

"I mean," Justine continued, "there's no need for a contest. I have plenty of excitement planned without it. The whole idea just seems really silly."

"That's what Niki says too," said Terry. "Niki, my girlfriend," he added quickly. "In fact, she won't have anything to do with the contest."

"Good for her," said Justine. "She's in my gym class, you know. Is it really true she's deaf? Someone told me she was, but it's hard to believe."

"It's true," said Terry. "But most people can't tell."

"I'm so glad she's coming to the party too," said Justine. "I don't have any close girlfriends in Shadyside, and I have a really special feeling about Niki."

"I'll tell her," said Terry. He left feeling warm inside. This party was really going to be special, he thought. And no one—not even Alex—was going to spoil it for him and Niki.

Niki was waiting at his locker when school was over. When she saw him walk up, she smiled sheepishly. "Hi, Terry," she said.

"Hi, Funny Face."

"I'm sorry I got so mad before," she said.

"It's okay," he said. "I'm sorry too. You were right.

I've been taking the contest too seriously. I promise from now on to just forget about it and relax."

"Good," said Niki.

Terry smiled at her. It was good to see her happy again. And he felt more relaxed than he had all week too. "So, which way should we walk home?" he asked. "The long way or the shortcut?"

"I think the long way would be nice, don't you?" said Niki, squeezing his hand.

"You bet," said Terry. The long way would mean an extra ten minutes of just the two of them alone together.

Terry stuffed his gear in his day pack. "Here, let me have your books," he told Niki.

She handed him her stack of books, but as she did, her geography book fell to the floor and a small scrap of paper fluttered out. Idly she picked it up and glanced at it, then gasped.

"What is it?" Terry took the paper from her. In crude block letters the note said:

YOU'LL WISH YOU WERE BLIND TOO.

chapter
_____
4

*I*ce.

Ice, Terry thought.

He felt frozen to the spot, chilled through. He felt as if he'd turned to ice.

And then he felt hot, hot with anger. "I can't believe someone would do such a cruel thing!" he said finally.

Niki didn't answer. She just stood there, obviously upset.

"There's only one person mean enough to do this," said Terry. "And you know who it is as well as I do."

"Don't start anything, Terry, please," said Niki.

"I haven't started anything, but I'm ready to finish something!" said Terry heatedly. "Alex is behind this. It can only be Alex."

"Terry, no, please don't!" Niki clutched his arm. "It wasn't Alex. Alex likes me. You're wrong. You're not thinking clearly."

"Listen, Niki, I know that—"

"You don't know who it was. If you say anything to Alex, it will only make things worse!"

"Yes, but I can't just—"

"Please," Niki repeated. "Let's just forget it."

"Forget it?" Terry was shocked that she could even suggest such a thing.

"It's—it's just a joke," she said. "It's mean, and stupid, but that's all it is. If we pretend it never happened, whoever did it won't get any satisfaction."

Terry could see that she was probably right, but he didn't like it. "Just not mention it?"

"Right," said Niki. "And not act upset."

"That's going to take an Academy Award–winning performance," said Terry.

"Please, Terry, for me," she said.

He looked down at her and felt himself melting. At times like this he knew that Niki was the most important person in his life, and he would do anything for her. "Okay, Funny Face," he said. "For you." She stood on her tiptoes and kissed him on the cheek.

"Thanks."

"In fact," Terry said, "I have an idea. Let's walk home by way of Pete's Pizza. We can practice our Academy Award performances over Cokes."

Niki smiled again, a genuine, loving smile. "You're on," she said.

Pete's Pizza was one of Shadyside's most popular teen hangouts, and that day it was jammed, both with kids from Shadyside and from the nearby junior college. Terry and Niki were lucky to find a tiny booth vacant.

While they waited for their orders, Terry started telling Niki about his biology project. It was so noisy in Pete's that he could barely hear anything she said, but she picked up everything he was telling her. He had just gotten to the part about how the seed splits into two when Niki interrupted him.

"Terry, look," she said, pointing.

He followed the direction of her finger and saw Justine standing in a phone booth, a serious look on her face.

"Maybe we ought to ask her to join us," Terry said. "She told me she wants to get to know you better."

"Okay," said Niki. "We'll just keep an eye on her and—" She stopped speaking and a strange expression came over her face.

Terry took her hand. "What's wrong? Niki, what is it?"

"Maybe nothing," said Niki. "But—look at Justine."

Terry turned to the phone booth again. Justine was still talking into the phone, with an odd, intense look. It was as if she'd changed into a different person, older, and cruel.

"I didn't mean to eavesdrop," Niki said. "But—I read her lips. And she said, 'They'll pay. Every one of them will pay.'"

chapter

5

Halloween Night

*T*he wind picked up, gusting wildly through the old cemetery, shaking the bare tree limbs like the bony fingers of skeletons. Niki squeezed Terry's hand as they approached the Cameron mansion. They were following Murphy, who was still chuckling over the scare he'd given them.

Suddenly Niki wheeled around. Two other kids were making their way through the cemetery, their costumes glowing in the pale, silvery October moonlight.

Everyone had been given directions to come the same way. They all had to park in the cul-de-sac at the end of Fear Street and cut through the cemetery to Justine's house at the edge of the woods.

In spite of the scare Murphy had given him and Niki, Terry decided that going through the cemetery had been a great idea. What could be better for putting everyone in a thrills-and-chills Halloween mood?

Up close, the Cameron mansion looked even spookier than it had from the cemetery. It was surrounded on both sides by barren trees that looked as if they must be hundreds of years old. The ground-floor windows were covered with heavy iron grates, and beside them battered wooden shutters banged in the wind.

They may be fixing this old house up, thought Terry, but it still resembles something out of a horror movie. Maybe it really *is* haunted. Just then there was a break in the wind, and he could hear music and shrieks of laughter from inside. It sounded as if the party had already started.

Murphy was clomping up the front steps to the porch, his zombie costume fluttering around him in the wind. Terry sneaked a quick glance at Niki and squeezed her hand reassuringly. She was dressed as an old-fashioned carnival reveler, in a beautiful red satin ball gown and flowing black cape. She had copied the dress from a book of old party costumes. She was beautiful. Grinning at Terry excitedly, she slid on her shiny black feathered eye mask.

Quickly Terry pulled on his own mask. His mother had helped him dress up as a greaser from the 1950s. He was wearing black chino pants and old saddle shoes of his father's that he'd found in the attic. He had rolled a pack of cigarettes in one sleeve of his tight white T-shirt and had a loose dark jacket over it. His hair was slicked back on the sides with Vaseline and teased up in the front. When he had left his house that evening, he'd thought he looked pretty cool, but now he wondered if he just looked silly.

Like a wimp.

As if reading his thoughts, Niki reached up and kissed him on the cheek. "You look great, Terry," she said.

Terry smiled down at her. "So do you, Funny Face." He slid up his mask and leaned over to kiss her. She kissed him back, and for a moment they just stood there, holding each other awkwardly because of their costumes, and kissing.

"Uh, Terry," Niki said after a moment. "What about the party?"

"What party?" said Terry. But he pulled away and smiled down at her again. Then, hand in hand, they mounted the steps up to the vine-choked porch. Murphy must have already gone inside, because the porch was empty.

There was a heavy, ornate door knocker in the shape of a skull in the center of the old wooden door. Terry reached out to pull it when suddenly a huge hairy spider swooped through the air and landed on his arm.

"No!"

Niki shrieked and Terry jumped back, his heart pounding.

"Gotcha again!"

Terry spun around and saw Murphy standing on the railing on the side of the porch, hidden by some of the vines. Cackling maniacally, Murphy jumped onto the porch. The giant rubber bug was on the end of a long pole and rubberband that he jerked up and down like a yo-yo.

Murphy laughed. "You two sure scare easy. If all the wimps are as wimpy as you, the jocks'll win this contest easy."

"Very funny, Murph," said Terry. He took a deep breath and then laughed.

Adjusting his mask, he raised his hand to knock again. There was a creaking noise, and the door slowly swung open.

Justine's living room was an eerie wonder, the ultimate fantasy of the ultimate Halloween dream—or nightmare. Artificial cobwebs hung in every corner, and cutouts of skeletons, witches, and bats dipped and swooped from the ceiling.

Along a narrow balcony above one side of the living room were colored spotlights that seemed to sweep the room in time to the music, their flickering lights causing everything to move eerily. The only other light came from the huge open fireplace, where a big black kettle was boiling, sending greenish fumes bubbling up.

All the furniture was from another century, but the music booming from hidden speakers was *now*. The whole effect was like the world's most modern haunted castle.

Even Murphy was impressed. "Wow," he said, stopping just inside the living room door. "I mean—wow!"

"Oh, Terry, it's excellent!" Niki gripped his arm in excitement.

They stood in the open door a moment as an apparition of beauty—or evil—crossed the room. It took Terry a moment to recognize Justine. She was dressed all in black, in a body-hugging, low-cut satin gown and high spiked sandals. Her thick blond hair was piled high on her head, and she had powdered her face and throat so they were dead white—except for a slash of red on her full lips and the glittering green irises of her eyes.

"She looks like the Bride of Frankenstein" Terry whispered.

Justine paused for effect, then smiled warmly. "Welcome to my crypt!" she said. "Almost everyone else is here. We were beginning to think the ghouls got you!"

"Great costume, Justine," said Niki.

"Thanks," said Justine. "I always wanted to be a vampire." She said it as if she meant it, then laughed. "Your costume's pretty cool too. It reminds me of one I saw at the Venice Carnivale."

"The what?" said Niki.   HINT 2

"A big party they hold in Venice once a year," said Justine. "Everyone dresses up and parties through the streets and canals. That's Venice, Italy," she added, "I used to live there with my ~~my~~ uncle. Which reminds me. Uncle Philip, I'd like you to meet my new friends."

A very skinny man stepped out of the shadows beside the fireplace. He was wearing a blue satin clown costume, and his face was covered with greasepaint in a sad clown mask. A single sparkling tear was glued below his right eye.

"This is Murphy Carter, Niki Meyer, and Terry Ryan," Justine said.

"I'm very pleased to meet all of you," said Philip, studying each one carefully with his sad clown eyes.

"We're very pleased to meet you," said Terry, shaking Philip's hand. "Your place is terrific."

"Yes," agreed Niki. "This is the most incredible party I've ever been to."

"Why, thank you," said Philip. "We had an engineer from Starflight Disco install the lights and sound system. Justine picked out all the tapes and CDs. We—my niece and I—have done all we could to make sure this is a party you will never forget."

"Let me take your coats," said Justine. "Come on in and join the fun. There's food over there on top of the casket, and soda chilling in that kettle."

Justine and her uncle left to talk to the other guests.

Terry remained by the door, checking out the fantastic decor. A couple of kids were dancing by the fireplace, and a few more were standing and eating and laughing. With all the decorations, the place looked like a movie set.

Justine and her uncle must have a lot of money, Terry thought. This party cost plenty. I wonder why she wanted to spend so much on just nine people?

"Pretty weird, huh?" said Niki at his side.

"Weird? Are you kidding! It's great!" exclaimed Terry.

"They've spent a lot of money on this party," Niki went on as if she had been reading his thoughts. "I wonder why she went to all this trouble?"

"Beats me," said Terry. "Maybe we're her favorite charity."

"Lucky us," said Niki. "Still—I'd like to know more about Justine."

Terry laughed. Niki was the most naturally curious person he'd ever known. "Hey, Funny Face," he said. "You can play Nancy Drew later. For now, let's check out the refreshments."

He took her hand and led her to the side of the room. As Justine had said, the refreshment "table" was a shiny black coffin. It was covered with an appetizing array of cheese, bread, crackers, and various dips and hors d'oeuvres, including several Terry had never seen before. A shelf above the coffin held huge bowls of chips and platters of pizza—pepperoni, onion, sausage, and every combination Terry had ever heard of. Below all the food was a huge black cauldron packed with ice and dozens of cans of soda.

"Look at this!" Terry said. "I've never seen so much food at a party."

"Me neither," Niki agreed, "except maybe when my parents have their New Year's party." She reached for a cracker covered with something pink. "Yummy!" she said. "I wonder what it is."

"Tarama salata," said Angela, who suddenly appeared beside her. She touched Niki's shoulder and repeated the words so Niki could read her lips. "It's a Greek dish made out of fish eggs. I asked Justine. She said she learned how to make it when she lived in the Greek islands."

"It's good," said Niki thoughtfully. "Try some, Terry."

"Fish eggs?" he said. "Thanks, anyway. I'll stick with pizza!" He stepped back and eyed Angela's costume appreciatively. She was dressed like a biker girl, all in leather, and had stenciled tattoos on her arms and neck. "Neat costume," he said.

"Thanks!" said Angela. "You should see some of the others. This is definitely the most excellent party I've ever been to."

While Niki sampled something green with white swirls in it, Terry munched on pizza and surveyed the rest of the party. It was a little hard to see with all the shadows, but he could make out Trisha and David talking in a corner underneath a human skull. David was wearing his basketball uniform, only instead of a basketball he was holding a big, round papier-mâché skull.

Trisha, her round face cheery and excited, was wearing a cheerleader's outfit from the fifties, with a tight pink sweater and short white skirt over white ankle-length boots. She had a big megaphone in her hand, and would have looked ridiculous, except she was obviously having such a good time.

In front of the fireplace Justine was dancing with Murphy: the vampire and the zombie. They looked gross, but also fascinating, like creatures out of a horror movie.

Terry was just wondering where the last couple of kids were when he heard a strange noise behind him. He turned and gawked, then started laughing. He couldn't help himself. It was Ricky Schorr, dressed as a frog.

He was wearing bright green long underwear, a pair of swim fins, and had a half mask on top of his head with bulging black eyes. "Ribit," he said.

"I don't believe this!" Terry finally said when he could breathe again. "You came as your biology project."

"You like it?" said Ricky, taking a swig of diet Dr Pepper. "I dyed the underwear myself. My mom got kind of upset, though—she couldn't get all the color out of her washing machine."

"I think it's the real you," said Angela nastily. "Sort of slimy and nerdy."

"Oh, yeah?" said Ricky. "That shows all you know. If you kiss me—I'll turn into a prince."

"I'll take my chances with the zombie, thanks," said Angela. Murphy and Justine had stopped dancing, and Angela walked over and took Murphy's hand.

"Hey, Funny Face," said Terry, touching Niki on the arm. "If you can stop eating for a couple of minutes—want to dance?"

A fast hip-hop song was on, and Niki closed her eyes a moment, to better sense the beat of the music, coming through vibrations in the floor. "Sure," she said. "I'd better stop eating anyway. Terry, this is the most fabulous food! She's got things here from Greece, Japan, France, Mexico. . . ."

"Not to mention good old American pizza," said Terry.

"Don't be a nerd," said Niki. She twirled away from him, then came back. "There's one thing I can't figure out," she said. "I don't see how Justine could possibly have lived in all those places. I mean, she's just a senior."

"Ask her later," said Terry. Another song started and they kept dancing. He watched Niki proudly. Niki was the prettiest girl there. Justine was too ghoulish, and Angela looked like a tramp, but Niki's red dress brought out the vibrant color in her cheeks and lips and made her dark eyes glow like coals.

To one side Ricky and Trisha danced, the bilious green frog and the cheerleader, both of them having a great time.

This is a cool party, Terry told himself. I still don't know why we were invited—but I'm glad.

The tape clicked off. While Philip went to change it, there was the sound of heavy knocking at the front door. Justine went to answer it, and everyone turned to see the late arrival.

For a moment there was total silence. Standing in the living room doorway, framed against the dark hallway, was a figure dressed in shining silver from head to toe.

He struck a pose, like a matador, then strode into the living room. Now Terry could see that it was Alex, dressed in a skin-tight silver body suit and a glittering silver mask. Beneath the silver his muscles rippled as he moved.

What a show-off, Terry thought.

Niki gripped Terry's hand tighter, and she whispered, "Wow! He looks fantastic!"

Several of the other guests began to whistle and shout.

Even Justine couldn't take her eyes off Alex. "Ladies and gentlemen," she said at last, "I give you—the Silver Prince!"

Alex came the rest of the way into the living room as if he owned it.

Terry couldn't resist saying something. Niki's exclamation of how fantastic Alex looked had set him off. "Hey, Alex," he called, "what are you supposed to be—the Tin Woodsman? Or is it Tinkerbell?"

Alex laughed. "Admit it, Ryan," he said. "You could never look this good in a million years."

Terry was still trying to think of a sarcastic reply when the music started up again, and for a moment

Alex danced by himself, the complete center of attention.

Niki tugged at Terry's arm. "Come on, Terry," she said. "Let's dance." She gave him such a loving look that for a moment Terry forgot to envy Alex's spectacular costume. Take that, Silver Prince, he thought. Show off all you want, but Niki wants to dance with *me*.

Even though she couldn't hear the sounds of the music, Niki was one of the best dancers Terry had ever known. She'd once explained to him how she felt the beat through her body, but he still wasn't sure how she did it.

All he knew was that he liked it. He felt as if he could dance like that forever, holding Niki close to him, the warmth of her body against his.

The slow song ended, and another started up, just as slow and romantic. Terry brushed Niki's hair with his lips, inhaling her spicy fragrance.

BAARRROOOOM.

The noise was as loud as a thunderclap.

"What was *that?*" someone yelled.

Everyone was startled.

The tape switched off.

"Hey—what's going on?"

In the next instant the room filled with smoke. Then the room filled with frightened cries, confused whispers.

No one was sure if it was a trick of some kind—or a catastrophe.

Terry was about to pull Niki toward the door when Justine stepped into the center of the room.

"Like my surprise?" she asked, her sexy body

almost disappearing in the smoke. "It's what they call a flash pot. My uncle Philip picked it up when he was a stage manager. I wanted to get your attention. Did I succeed?"

A couple of kids cheered and clapped. A few were still too stunned to react.

Justine smiled, then raised an eyebrow. "I promised you lots of surprises," she said. "And there will be more to come. But for now—who's up for more dancing?"

The cheers and applause grew even louder. Terry found himself cheering too. It seemed that anything could happen at this party, and he was ready for it.

"Good," said Justine. "But first I have to tell you a true story. Throughout history people have loved to dance. But in the Middle Ages dancing was sometimes much more than just fun. In fact, some people were said to be taken by evil spirits when they danced. They would dance faster and faster, faster and faster, till they literally danced themselves to death. I don't know if we have evil spirits here tonight, but anything can happen on Halloween. Is anyone brave enough to try some really fast music?"

"Yeah!"

"Let's go!"

"Yo!"

The crowd was now ready for anything. If Justine had told them all to jump into a swimming pool with their clothes on, Terry thought, they would have done it.

"We'll see how fast you can go!" Justine said. She reached behind her and flicked a switch. The candles on the wall went out. At the same time a strobe light came on, and the music came back on, loud and fast, a relentless synthesized rhythm, over electronic-sounding voices repeating "Get your freak on, get your freak on," over and over.

The fire in the fireplace had died down to embers, so the only light came from the strobe. In its rapid flickering everything seemed to move faster and faster.

Terry took Niki's hands and twirled her. Everyone was laughing, dancing, shouting, and changing partners. In the eerie light it was hard to see who was dancing with whom. Once Terry found himself dancing with Ricky!

It was fun, but it went on and on. Whenever Terry started to slow down, the music went faster.

In the center of the room Alex was twirling like a shiny silver top, and Terry suddenly wondered where Niki was. Just when he spotted her, dancing with David, the lights went out. The tape player died down with a sad groan.

For a moment there was dead silence. Except for the faint glow from the fireplace the room was in total darkness.

"What is this, Justine, another surprise?" asked Murphy's voice after a moment.

"I don't know what happened," said Justine. She sounded a little frightened. "Uncle Philip—"

"I'll check the fuse box," Philip's voice said calmly. "Don't go away."

"Don't worry, everyone," said Justine, still sounding scared. "We just had a new electric system installed, and the strobe must have overheated it. My uncle will change the fuses, and we'll—"

At that moment the artificial candles came back on and the tape started up again.

But no one felt like dancing anymore because the light showed a horrifying sight.

In front of the fireplace, half on and half off the rug, lay a limp body.

Blood trickled down its sides from the huge carving knife sticking out of its back.

chapter
6

For a moment nobody moved or spoke. Then several people began screaming at once. Terry's heart was beating so fast he could hear it. The vast room seemed to spin, then tilt. He grabbed a chair back to steady himself.

It took a while for his head to clear. Sounds came back. He could hear individual voices.

"Oh, no, no!"

"Is it real?"

"Who is it?"

"Somebody—call 911."

Tightly holding Niki's hand, Terry began to move toward the body with the other guests. He could see now that it was someone dressed in a skeleton costume. But who?

Everyone seemed reluctant to get any nearer. Finally Alex squatted down. He tentatively reached out to touch the body when suddenly the skeleton jumped up.

"Trick or treat!" the skeleton yelled, and collapsed, laughing uncontrollably, back on the rug.

It was Les Whittle.

There were gasps of surprise.

Then laughter, nervous at first, built until the room nearly shook from it.

"One for the *wimp* side!" shouted Ricky in triumph.

"Great trick, Les!" Terry clapped him on the shoulder.

"It *was* good," agreed Trisha in a shaky voice, "but you had us *all* scared to death. Why didn't you tell the rest of the team you were going to do it?"

"Because Justine and I didn't cook it up till just this morning," said Les, still laughing. He showed them all the knife. It was just a knife handle. The "blood" was the kind that comes in a tube. "I found these in a joke shop and thought it would be a shame to waste them," he explained. "It was the easiest thing in the world."

"Yeah, well, for your information none of us was scared at all," said Murphy. "That's just the sort of wimpy trick a wimp would pull."

Les wasn't at all perturbed. "Sure, Murph. Tell us another one," he said, chuckling. He put his horn-rimmed glasses on over his skeleton mask. It made him appear incongruous, like a studious corpse. "I've been hiding in the kitchen for half an hour," he said. "Where's the food? I'm starved!"

Most of the kids, exhausted by dancing and the scare, collapsed on the antique furniture, eating and talking.

"What a dumb trick!" said David, his legs thrown over the arm of an antique rocking chair.

"You're just jealous 'cause you didn't think of it," said Trisha.

"We've thought of better tricks," David said. "Much better. You'll see what I mean, unless you get some sense and go home now."

"Never!" said Ricky. "You jocks don't have a chance!"

"You're the ones who don't have a chance," said Alex. "But I gotta hand it to Les. He made a pretty good corpse."

Terry didn't say anything. Niki was sitting, turned away from everyone, eating another plateful of food. He was glad she couldn't hear the conversation, because it would probably just get her mad again.

"So what do you think, guys?" asked Alex jovially, sitting next to Terry and Niki on the arm of an antique wooden bench. "Think your team can go the distance?"

"We've got a better chance than your team," muttered Terry. "We have some brains on our side."

Alex laughed. He wanted it to sound like a good-natured laugh, but Terry knew better.

"Great costume, Niki," Alex said, admiring her appreciatively.

"Thanks," Niki said. "I made it myself."

"You always could do anything," said Alex. "I remember that great dress you made for the freshman dance. You were the best-looking girl there."

"Well, thanks," said Niki. Her eyes were sparkling, and Terry forced himself to take a slow, deep breath. He hated himself for feeling jealous, but he couldn't help it.

After all, Niki was sitting next to *him,* holding *his* hand, so why did he feel so jealous of Alex?

Why did he want to punch him in the face?

"Say, Niki," said Alex teasingly, "don't you think it's about time you joined the jock team?"

Niki's eyes changed. She was no longer flirtatious, but sad now—and a little angry. "Oh, will you two stop it with your idiotic games? I've said a hundred times I'm not on either side!"

She abruptly stood up and walked toward the fireplace.

The dance music had started again, and Terry was surprised to see Niki ask Ricky to dance.

"What's with her?" Alex asked Terry. "I guess she's been hanging out with you for so long, she's forgotten how to take a joke."

"Hey, Beale, you're the joke," Terry muttered. "She just doesn't like the whole contest idea."

"Hey, man, I thought you were supposed to be such a good talker. You know, debate team and everything. And you mean you couldn't talk Niki into joining your team? Whoa!"

"Niki makes her own decisions." Terry stood up. "I don't own her."

"Wow. Heavy talk, Ryan. Back off, okay?" Alex leaned away from Terry and put up his hands as if shielding himself. "You and I used to be friends, remember?"

Used to be, Terry thought. Those are the key words.

He realized that Alex was reaching out to him. Alex was deliberately reminding him of what good buddies they had been until very recently.

Alex was staring at him expectantly, but Terry couldn't respond. He just had a bad feeling about

Alex. He couldn't pretend to want him as a friend again.

Alex's eyes filled with disappointment. "Later, man," he said abruptly, and got up quickly from the bench.

Alex walked toward the glowing fireplace with a swagger. The song on the tape ended. Alex stepped up to Niki and Ricky and smoothly took Niki's hand.

As if he owns it or something, Terry thought, watching with growing discomfort.

Trying not to look as if he were watching, Terry kept sneaking glances at Alex and Niki. They were dancing to a fast number, and Niki was smiling.

Does she have to smile? Terry asked himself. Maybe he should go over and interrupt them. But that would just make Niki angry, and Terry really didn't want any kind of confrontation with Alex.

He watched some of the others for a while. Ricky and Trisha were dancing together again. While he watched, Ricky said something that made Trisha laugh so hard she almost fell over.

David was dancing with Angela. He was a pretty good dancer, and Terry realized that he didn't really know David. He was quieter than the other jocks and didn't seem to take the competition as seriously as the rest of them did.

The song ended and another began. Niki was still dancing with Alex. Enough is enough, Terry told himself. He started to cross to them when a musical voice stopped him.

"Going somewhere?"

Terry twisted around to see Justine standing behind a loveseat.

"I, uh, thought I'd dance," said Terry.

"Isn't that a coincidence?" said Justine. "I was just thinking the same thing. How about dancing with me?" She gave him her warmest smile, and Terry felt the knot in his stomach start to dissolve.

"Well sure," he said. I'd love to."

"Good," said Justine. She took his hand and led him over near the fireplace. A slow tune was playing on the stereo. Terry saw Niki whirl past with Alex, the Silver Prince, but she didn't see him.

Up close Terry became very aware of Justine's animal warmth and her perfume, a faint musky scent different from anything he had smelled before. She settled even closer, pressing her body tightly against his.

"How are you enjoying the party?" she asked huskily.

"It's great," he said sincerely. "I think everyone is really in a party mood now."

"Good," said Justine. "It's very important to me for all of you to enjoy yourselves."

"Everything's perfect," Terry said, talking to distract himself from the way he was feeling. "The food, the music, the lights. You've thought of everything. You and your uncle."

"As a matter of fact, Uncle Philip's up in the attic now," she said, "preparing a few extra surprises."

"How'd you ever dream all this stuff up?" Terry asked.

"We've had a long time to think about it," said Justine. "But enough questions. Let's just enjoy the music—and each other."

She pressed even closer to him, and for a moment Terry forgot everything except the scent and closeness of Justine.

The tape ended and the dancers broke apart. Justine squeezed Terry's hand and went to put on a new tape.

Guiltily, Terry realized that Niki was standing by the fire, staring at him. She didn't look jealous, or even angry, but there was a strange, unreadable expression on her face.

Alex said something to her, and Niki shook her head. She started to cross over to where Terry was, but stopped suddenly, her eyes wide with surprise.

Everyone heard a tremendous thumping at the door—along with a growling roar from farther away.

The noise was so intense that Niki picked up the vibrations. Her mouth dropped open and she turned toward the front of the room.

Ricky pulled open the door, and the roaring became a deafening blast of sound.

Then, as everyone watched in shock, two gleaming motorcycles bombed right into the living room!

chapter

7

All Terry and the others could do at first was stare in shock at the motorcycles. The riders were dressed in leather jackets and pants, and their faces were completely covered with shiny black helmets.

"Oh, wow!" someone yelled over the thunderous noise.

"Rad! Really rad!" Ricky shouted, his idea of a funny comment.

The whole crazy scene reminded Terry of the movie *Animal House,* which he and Niki had rented a few weeks before. That movie had a guy riding a motorcycle up and down the stairs.

Was this another of Justine's "surprises"? Terry wondered, enjoying the crazy, chaotic scene.

With a final roar, the two bikers cut their machines. The sudden quiet was almost deafening.

The bigger of the two riders removed his helmet

and got off the bike. With a sinking feeling, Terry saw that it was Bobby McCorey. Bobby's eyes were bloodshot and he had a nasty expression on his face. "Nice party," he said sarcastically.

"Yeah," agreed Marty Danforth, the other rider. He twirled his helmet in his hands as he checked out the room. "Great place you got here. Too bad we had to knock so loud."

"For some reason the door was locked," Bobby added. "It's almost like you didn't want us."

Justine stepped forward, her face a mask of fury. "Get out of here," she said in an icy voice.

"Get out?" said Bobby. "We just got here."

"I told you you weren't invited," Justine said. She didn't sound frightened at all, Terry noticed, but was so angry her voice was shaking.

"Yeah, well, we told you we don't like to be left out of things," Bobby said, forcing a tough-guy sneer on his face.

Now Philip stepped quickly to the center of the room. "Who are these young men?" he asked Justine.

"Two clowns from the high school," Justine told him. "They're not on the list."

Philip approached Bobby and Marty. He had an expression on his face like a teacher who was disappointed with his class. Terry could see that Philip didn't realize how mean Bobby and Marty could be.

"If you leave right now," said Philip, "I won't call the police."

"Hear that?" Marty asked Bobby, his sneer frozen in place like a bad Elvis imitator. "He won't call the police." Both boys laughed.

"Don't do us any favors, man," said Bobby, and he

shoved Philip, hard, in the chest. With a gasp Philip fell backward and banged into a table.

"Uncle Philip!" cried Justine in horror. Several of the kids rushed to Philip's aid. Niki, her dark eyes wide with fright, ran to Terry, gripping his hand.

"Sorry about that. It was an accident," Bobby said, slurring his words. He stumbled over a floorboard, and Terry realized he'd been drinking.

By now the other kids were recovering from the shock of the bikers' entrance. "Go home!" several shouted. "Get out of here, you creeps!"

Bobby and Marty ignored the others. "Nice place they got here," said Bobby. "Kinda looks like your place, huh, Marty?"

They both laughed as if Bobby had just made a hilarious joke.

"Why don't we help 'em out a little and clear away some of the cobwebs," said Marty. He unhooked a chain from one of his belt loops and, with a flick of his wrist, swung it at the cutouts over the fireplace. Instantly they fell to the floor in tatters.

Terry stared in disbelief. Why didn't someone *do* something? Now Marty started to wreck the decorations over the window.

Terry couldn't stand it anymore. "Hey, man, don't *do* that!" he said.

He took a step toward Marty, but Bobby moved faster. Terry felt his head jerk back as if he'd just been hit by a truck. The next thing he knew he was on his back, with Niki's face, very close and frightened looking, gazing down at him.

He tried to sit up, but Niki pushed him back down. "Don't try to move," she whispered.

"Uh-oh. The skinny guy tripped," Bobby said,

grinning. He stared at the Others menacingly. "Hope nobody else trips—or anything."

Marty laughed. They slapped each other high-fives with their black-gloved hands.

These guys sure know how to have a good time, thought Terry. Whatever they'd been drinking or smoking had made them think they were hilarious.

Justine stepped forward again. She was still angry, but Terry saw that now she was also frightened.

"All right, guys," she said. "So I made a mistake. I was wrong not to invite you to the party. But everything was planned for the nine people who are already here. If you'll just leave now, I promise I'll have a special party—just for you—next week."

"Hey, that's okay," said Bobby. "We're having a great time. Don't sweat it." He walked over to the food. Ricky, Angela, and Trisha, who had been standing there, quickly edged away.

Bobby took a big bite of one of the hors d'oeuvres, then spat it out. "Yuck!" he bellowed. "What is this stuff? It tastes like fish!" He turned angrily to Justine. "Haven't you got any real food here? Chips? Pizza?"

"There's plenty of pizza on the shelf over there," said Justine. "Take what you want and—"

"What about drinks?" interrupted Marty. "All I see here is kid stuff." He turned to Philip, who was sitting on a low stool now, looking sick. "Where do you keep the beer, man?" Marty asked.

"I don't drink," said Philip curtly. "I never keep alcohol in the house."

"I don't believe you," said Marty. "What kinda host are you? My friend and I are thirsty." He grabbed Philip by his lapels.

"Stop it!"

Alex's sudden yell stopped Marty for a moment. Like a silver streak, Alex crossed the room and grabbed Marty, pulling him away from Philip.

Marty bellowed in rage. Alex's triumph was short-lived. A moment later Bobby grabbed Alex from behind, then held on to him while Marty kicked him, hard, in the stomach.

"Ohhh."

With a gasp of pain Alex fell to the floor and lay curled in a ball, gasping for breath.

"Oh, man. Another accident," said Bobby, stepping over Alex.

While the guests looked on helplessly, Bobby and Marty began to ransack the beautiful old living room, opening doors and cabinets and throwing everything they found onto the floor.

Whenever anyone made a move to stop them, Bobby twirled his chain menacingly. They found a bottle of red wine somewhere and began trading it back and forth.

This has got to stop, Terry told himself. They may be tough, but we've got them outnumbered.

Across the room David caught his eye and nodded in the direction of the cycles. Terry nodded back and slowly got up and began to inch toward the machines. Casually he picked up a heavy candlestick from an end table. Niki looked at him, her eyes wide with fright. "It's okay," he mouthed soundlessly.

Bobby and Marty were so busy eating and ransacking the room that they didn't notice Terry and David on their bikes until the air filled with the sound of the engines revving up.

"Hey!" Both Bobby and Marty forgot what they

were doing and leapt for the bikes. "Leave those alone!"

But Terry and David were ready for them. Just as the two bikers reached the motorcycles, Terry and David jumped off the seats. Bobby and Marty dived for the two boys, but came up with nothing but air.

With a bellow of rage, Marty stood up and swung his chain at Terry.

Terry caught the end of it with the candlestick. He pulled, and Marty cried out in anger and pain as the chain twisted out of his hand.

Meanwhile, David and Bobby were fighting, rolling over and over on the floor. Bobby was a dirty fighter, but he was half drunk, and David was quicker. He had Bobby down and was pounding his face, causing blood to spurt over both of them. With another blow he stunned Bobby, then stood up, satisfied.

Marty had forgotten about his chain and advanced on Terry threateningly, wildly swinging his fists at him.

Terry kept ducking and moving backward, searching for an opening, a way to stop him. From the corner of his eye he saw David suddenly mount Marty's bike, turn it around, and gun it out the front door. He jumped off at the last minute.

"Hey, Marty," David called. "Your bike's gone home without you!"

Marty looked around in horror, then turned and ran out after his runaway bike.

A second later there was a sickening crash.

"How about we do the same thing to your bike?" Terry said to Bobby, who was just struggling up from the floor.

Without a word, Bobby threw a leg over his bike, his face a bloody mess.

"Tough guys, huh?" Bobby sneered. He glared at Terry first and then David with such hatred that Terry felt his stomach turn over. "You're dead meat, man. You're history. Both of you."

He looked around the room slowly, menacingly. "Later," he said.

With a final threatening look, he gunned the motorcycle and rode out of the mansion and into the night.

chapter
8

The smell of motorcycle exhaust hung in the air. Several kids began congratulating Terry and David on getting rid of the two bikers, but their thanks were subdued. Everyone seemed to be in shock.

"Nice going," Murphy said.

"We did what we had to," said David, wiping his bloody face with a tissue. "Maybe they'll go pick on someone else for a while."

"Justine, where's your phone?" said Terry. "We've got to report this to the police."

Panic and alarm crossed Justine's face. "No! No police."

"But they broke into your house!" said David. "They vandalized it! And you heard their threats."

"That's all they were—just threats," Justine said. She moved closer to David, put a hand on his arm, and stared directly into his face. "Those boys are bullies," she said. "All swagger and no substance. They wouldn't dare come back after the way you and Terry faced them down."

"Well, I don't know," David said uncertainly.

"Really, everything's fine now," said Justine. "A few of the decorations are ruined, but so what? What's important is that no one was really hurt. Alex? Terry? Are you all right?"

"Fine," muttered Alex.

"I'm okay," said Terry. His cheek hurt where Bobby had punched him, and he suspected there would be a big bruise, but no real harm had been done.

"Thank you, all of you, for being so brave," Justine said, turning her smile up to full wattage. A look of mischief crossed her face, and then she added, "Now are you brave enough for the next surprise?"

"You mean we're just going to keep going as if nothing happened?" said Angela.

"Well, I hope so," said Justine. "If we stop now, Bobby and Marty will have won. Besides," she added, her lovely face turning pouty, "I've worked so hard planning everything. We haven't even had half the surprises yet."

"We also haven't settled things between the jocks and the wimps," added Murphy Carter. "Of course, if you wimps want to concede defeat now—"

"No way!" said Ricky. "We're just as game as you guys. And for your information, our team has a few more tricks up its sleeve."

"Good," said Justine. "Then it's settled. Why don't you all relax for a while. I'll bring out more food. And then in a few minutes we can start the treasure hunt."

She disappeared in the direction of the kitchen.

Terry was starting to get his second wind and wondered what Justine's next surprise could be. He sneaked a glance at Alex, who was leaning against the wall beside the fireplace, fully recovered from his injury.

Alex caught his eye and shrugged. Then he mouthed one word: *wimp.* Terry knew he had to stay on his toes. Alex was still into this dumb contest. That meant Terry had to be too. No way Alex was going to win, after everything that had happened.

Justine and Philip brought out trays with hot apple cider and cookies, and soon everyone was relaxed and in a party mood again.

The tape machine was playing golden oldies from the fifties, and Trisha and Ricky began dancing to "At the Hop." Trisha was smiling and seemed happy again.

"I love these old songs!" Angela said, clapping in time to the music. She leaned back against a corner of the stone fireplace, then gave a little shriek as it shifted and opened.

Where the solid stones had been—was a human skeleton, its hollow face grinning mindlessly.

There were several screams and then the sound of laughter as everyone realized it was another "surprise."

"I see you've discovered one of our trapdoors," Justine said with her smile.

"One of them?" said Angela. "You mean there are more?"

"Remember," said Justine. "I promised a lot of surprises."

"Sweet," said Angela.

"How you doing, Funny Face?" Terry turned to Niki, who was leaning back against the cushions on the sofa beside him, sipping cider.

"Okay," she said. "How are *you?*" She gently touched his cheek where Bobby had hit him.

"I'm okay," he said. "I just hope Bobby and Marty don't—"

He was cut off by a surprised shriek.

"What *is* that?" protested Angela, her face twisted in disgust.

"Human brain," said Ricky. He was standing in front of her, innocently holding a dark metal box.

"Get real!" said Alex. "Where would you get a human brain?"

"From my uncle," said Ricky, still innocent. "He runs a medical supply house. He let me borrow it for the party."

Angela looked as if she was going to be sick.

"Let me see that!" Murphy said.

"I can't take it out—we'd ruin it," said Ricky, holding the box tighter. "Of course, if you want to *touch* it—"

Alex defiantly thrust his hand into the box, then just as quickly pulled it out with a strangled cry.

"Sort of slimy, isn't it?" said Ricky smugly. "Anyone else want to try?"

"Sure," said David. He walked up to Ricky, pretended to put his hand in the box, but grabbed it instead and turned it upside down. The contents slithered out, landing on the stone hearth with a sickening *plop.*

"Some brains!" said David. "Looks like cold spaghetti to me. Gotcha!"

"No, I gotcha first," said Ricky. "Angela and Alex both thought it was brains."

"No, we didn't," protested Alex. "We were just putting you on. This is one for the jock team—"

The argument about whose gotcha it was stopped when Justine rang a little bell.

"May I have your attention?" She was standing in front of the fire, and outlined in light it was almost possible to believe she *was* a vampire. To one side of the fireplace her uncle Philip sat slouched on a stool, the artificial tear sparkling on his sad clown's face.

"Is everyone back in the groove, ready to party?" Justine asked. Without waiting for an answer, she went on. "It's time for the next surprise. This one is a treasure hunt, but it's not like any treasure hunt you've ever heard of."

"A treasure hunt!" exclaimed Trisha. "What fun!"

"Get real," said Murphy. "Treasure hunts are for little kids—and wimps."

Justine, still smiling, turned to Murphy. "You might not think so when you see the list of items," she said teasingly. "But, of course, no one has to participate. In fact, it could be a little dangerous. This treasure hunt is only for those who are *really* brave."

"Hey, I never said I wouldn't participate," said Murphy.

"Good," said Justine, her cat-green eyes sparkling with excitement. She began passing out a photocopied list. "This is a list of the items Uncle Philip and I have hidden around the mansion," she went on. "There are treasures in every room—on both floors and in the attic and basement. Whichever team finds the most treasures by midnight will win a special prize."

Everyone grabbed the lists and prepared to rush off—but Justine's voice stopped them. "One more thing," she added. "Please be careful. After all—anything can happen on Halloween."

Trisha found the first treasure before anyone had even left the living room. While Justine was still explaining the rules, Trisha carefully removed the food still sitting on the casket and opened it to reveal a bundle of bones wrapped in tattered blue cloth. The hand bones of a mummy.

"I've got a treasure!" she cried. "But, Justine, is this really from a mummy?"

"Supposedly," said Justine. "We picked it up in Egypt."

For the next few minutes everyone checked out the ground floor. There were constant shrieks and laughter as one person after another discovered a new treasure—or a trick.

"This is great, isn't it?" said David, laughing, as he and Terry simultaneously walked into the pantry from opposite doors.

"I can't believe all this weird stuff Justine and her uncle have," Terry said. He showed David the only treasure he'd found so far—a hairy tarantula preserved in a glass paperweight. "I found this in the toilet tank."

"I found my treasure in a terrarium," David said, showing Terry a stuffed cobra. "At first I thought it was alive because it was moving around. But then I saw it was attached to an electric motor."

"I'm not even sure I want to find some of this stuff," Terry said, scanning his list. "A bottle of blood?"

"Murphy already found that," David said. "He was

66

prowling around in the front hall and tripped over a loose floorboard. The bottle was right under it."

"Catch you later," Terry said. David was a good guy, he realized. Too bad the other jocks weren't more like him. The thought of the jocks made him think of Alex, which made him think of Niki, and he wondered where she was in this big spooky house. Maybe he'd run into her.

Niki looked at the list halfheartedly. Even though this was the greatest party she'd ever been to, she wasn't that interested in fun and games.

The party still seemed like a mystery to her. Nothing added up. The treasure hunt, she decided, was the perfect chance to explore the mansion freely.

She replayed in her mind the conversation she had lip-read when Justine was in the phone booth, and had now decided that it didn't have anything to do with the party.

After all, Justine seemed only to care about her guests having a good time. And despite her weird uncle, she was really sweet.

But there was still something intriguing about her, and Niki was determined to find out what it was. She would have felt a little guilty about searching the house, but the treasure hunt gave her the perfect excuse. It wasn't even snooping, not really. . . .

She was working her way through the rooms on the top floor. So far none of them contained anything of interest to her.

She entered a large bedroom at the back of the house and switched on the light. She jumped back, her heart pounding, as a huge glowing head dropped in front of her. After a second she realized it was just another one of Justine's surprises.

She switched the light off again, and the head was pulled back up to the ceiling on an automatic reel. After a little searching she found a lamp and clicked it on, then smiled in satisfaction.

From the perfume bottles and cosmetics on the antique vanity and the beautiful ruffled pink satin bedspread, she realized she must be in Justine's room.

You can tell a lot about a person by examining her bedroom, Niki thought. For example, take her own bedroom. Her sewing stuff and the fashion cutouts on the bulletin board showed her interest in fashion design. Her collection of stuffed dogs showed that she loved animals and hoped someday to raise them. And her rock posters showed just the sort of music she preferred.

But, she realized, standing in the middle of Justine's room, this room didn't say much about Justine at all. There were no stuffed animals, no pictures of movie actors or rock stars, no hint of a hobby, nothing personal at all, except for a picture of a smiling man and woman from the fifties in an ornate frame on the vanity.

Justine's schoolbooks were stacked on top of the radiator, but there was nothing in the room that could be used as a desk.

Strange, Niki thought. Justine must not take school very seriously. But then, she reminded herself, after all the places she's lived, Shadyside must seem like very small potatoes.

She opened each of the drawers in a chest, but there

wasn't much in them besides a few folded pairs of underpants and some sweaters.

Her curiosity piqued even more—by what she *hadn't* found—Niki opened the closet door and was shocked to find it almost empty, except for the school clothes she'd seen Justine in.

Where were her jeans, sweatshirts, sneakers? What did she wear after school? Didn't she have any party dresses?

She took her flashlight, shone it around the closet, then saw a faint, square-shaped crack at the back. She remembered the trapdoor in the fireplace and wondered if this was another one.

Excited, she stepped to the back of the closet and began to press around the crack with her fingertips. Nothing happened.

Frowning, Niki stared at the door, then began to feel around the empty closet shelves. Her finger touched a small knob and she turned it. The back of the closet swung open, revealing another, larger closet.

Niki gasped in surprise.

This hidden closet was jammed with clothing—but clothing very different from the everyday clothes she had seen. At first she thought they might be very old clothes left by the people who had lived in the Cameron mansion before.

But when she took a few off the hangers, she saw that they were new, many of them with labels from expensive designers and famous department stores in New York, San Francisco, and Paris.

There were beautiful woolen suits, shiny satin cocktail dresses, colorful skirts and jackets in sophisticated styles that no one she knew would wear. A chrome rack on the floor held dozens of beautiful high-heeled shoes in every type of leather and every color of the rainbow.

The back of the closet revealed three beautiful full-length formal gowns and two fur coats, one mink and one fox.

Niki couldn't believe her eyes. This was the most beautiful wardrobe she had ever seen. Were all these clothes Justine's? But when would she wear them? And why were they hidden away like this?

Maybe, she decided, they were Justine's mother's clothes. But nobody really knew if Justine had a mother or not. Maybe there was another, older woman who lived here—Philip's girlfriend or wife, maybe? But in that case, why did Justine have so few clothes of her own?

It's a real mystery, Niki thought. She loved mysteries.

A small bureau stood against one side of the closet and Niki opened its drawers to reveal pastel negligees, nightgowns, and silk underwear. In the bottom drawer was a carefully wrapped package. She opened it, not even considering that someone might catch her snooping, and was shocked to see a framed photo of Justine and a man with their arms around each other, gazing lovingly into each other's eyes. But the man was much older—from the streaks of gray in his hair, at least forty.

Was Justine having an affair with an older man? Was that why she never went out with the boys from school or never went to any of the games?

Niki carefully put everything back just the way she had found it, then closed the secret door. She was about to leave Justine's room when her eye caught the bathroom door.

She went in and, with only a small pang of conscience, opened the medicine chest. It was filled with typical medicine-cabinet things: toothpaste, mouthwash, several bottles of nail polish and other cosmetics, aspirin, and a box of Band-Aids.

There were three prescription bottles on the top shelf. Niki took them down one by one. She didn't recognize the names of any of the medications, except a sleeping pill her mother sometimes used. But all three prescriptions were made out to "Enid Cameron."

Enid? Niki thought. Who's Enid? Philip's wife?

But no matter how many explanations she considered, the one that kept popping into her mind was that Justine was somehow leading a double life.

During the day she went to school like any other teenager. But at night and on weekends she had a whole other life that no one else knew anything about.

But why? And why keep it all such a secret?

Maybe, Niki thought, she was just letting her imagination run away with her. Maybe there was a logical explanation for everything she had seen. She needed to talk to Terry, she realized. If anyone could figure this puzzle out, it was him.

Now all she had to do was find him, somewhere in the mansion.

Terry was really enjoying the treasure hunt. So far, in addition to the tarantula, he'd found three of the items on the list: a polished monkey skull that had been hidden inside a laundry hamper, a crystal ball, and his latest acquisition, an ivory pendant in the shape of a dagger.

He found the pendant when he had opened a cupboard and was scared out of his wits by what appeared to be a bloody, disembodied head—but turned out, on closer inspection, to be the head of a mannequin, covered with catsup.

After he had got over his fright, Terry found the pendant around the mannequin's neck. He'd laughed and added it to the rest of his loot.

He heard a couple of other treasure hunters coming his way, then remembered that Justine had said her uncle Philip was preparing some surprises in the attic. He searched and found a narrow staircase leading upstairs.

Mounting the dark, creaky stairs to the attic, his heart thudded with anticipation and a little thrill of fear. What treasures would he find up there? What scares? This was definitely the best party he'd ever been to.

The attic was small and dusty, and filled with old boxes and trunks. Terry realized, from the thick layer of dust on the boxes and trunks, that they had been sealed up long ago.

He switched on the overhead light and spotted a closet door. A perfect place to hide items on the list, he thought.

Grinning to himself, Terry pulled open the door, then stopped and stared in shock.

"No! Oh, please—*no!*"

The room went white. Terry's breath caught in his throat.

He gripped the closet door to hold himself up and stared into the shadowy cubicle.

"Alex? Alex?" he cried.

Hanging from a rope was the limp body of the Silver Prince, his neck bent at an impossible angle. Sticky red blood was splattered over the front of the beautiful costume. It puddled onto the closet floor.

Drip, drip, drip . . .

chapter

9

*I*t's another trick, Terry told himself.

Please. Oh, please—let it be another trick.

But the silver costume was real. And the blood continued to drip as he watched.

Drip, drip, drip.

A steady rhythm he knew he'd remember for the rest of his life.

He was still staring at the bent form of his friend, trying to get the strength to go for someone, when he heard a voice behind him. "Whatcha got—oh, no!"

It was David, horror on his face.

"I just found him," Terry said, his voice and hands shaking. "Maybe it's another trick."

"I don't think so," said David. "Don't touch him. I'll go for help."

"I'm coming with you." Terry didn't want to spend another second with Alex's corpse.

On the way down the stairs they ran into Ricky,

Trisha, and Les. Quickly David told them what Terry had found.

"We've got to call an ambulance!" said Trisha. "Maybe he's only hurt."

"It's more than that," said David. "You didn't see him. His neck—all the blood . . ."

Terry shuddered, remembering the ruined costume. He had had his problems with Alex, sure, but no one deserved to have something so terrible happen to him.

"At least call the police!" said Les.

"First let's tell Justine and her uncle what happened," said David. "They'll know what to do."

Justine and her uncle were sitting in front of the fireplace, talking together in low tones. When the frightened guests burst into the living room and explained what had happened, Justine jumped up at once, concern radiating from her lovely face.

"You call the police," Philip told Justine. "I'll see what the situation is."

"Wait, Uncle Philip!" said Justine. "No police—yet." Philip nodded and together with the others they ran up the two flights of stairs to the attic.

"It's in here," said Terry, leading the others to the closet. He braced himself for what he knew he was going to see and pulled open the door.

There was nothing at all inside the closet.

"I don't believe this!" he cried.

"Where is he?" asked David at the same moment.

"Very funny," said Trisha angrily. "For your information, Terry, you're not supposed to pull tricks on members of your *own team!*"

"It's not a trick!" Terry protested. "I saw him—we both did!"

"He was here," David added. "And blood was

dripping." He bent down and touched the closet floor. "It's dry," he said, sounding astonished.

"I guess I'm not the only one who prepares 'surprises,' " said Justine with a little smile. "Come on, Uncle Philip, let's go back downstairs."

The others were about to follow them when Niki came into the room.

"Has anyone seen Terry?" she asked. Then she spotted him. "What's going on? What are all of you doing in here?"

Quickly the others explained what had happened. "So we get up here," Les finished, "and there's not only no body, the closet's completely empty. Obviously, they made the whole thing up."

"Did you make it up?" Niki asked Terry, her dark eyes searching his face.

"No," Terry repeated. "I saw the body. It was real. I don't know where it is now, but it was here."

"Come to think of it," said Ricky, starting to sound worried, "I haven't seen Alex for quite a while. Has anyone?"

"Maybe you just thought you saw something," said Niki. "There are a lot of shadows in here."

"What we saw was real," said David. "It was Alex."

"Then if he was—like you say— We've got to find him!" said Niki. "Come on, Terry, let's look in the rest of the rooms."

No one felt like searching alone, so the six of them—Terry, Niki, Les, David, Ricky, and Trisha—carefully checked behind the boxes in the attic, then crept down the stairs and began to go through the rooms on the second floor.

"This is Justine's room," said Niki, opening the door. "Maybe he just—" She broke off with a shriek.

76

The others crowded closer. Lying on Justine's bed was the Silver Prince.

But as soon as they got near, it became clear it wasn't Alex.

Ricky approached the bed first. "Hey!" he said. "This is just—"

"A dummy!" Terry finished for him. The object lying on the bed was Alex's silver costume, stuffed full of rags. The "blood" Terry and David had seen was streamers of red cellophane that had moved slightly to resemble dripping. In that light it was hard for Terry to believe he had been fooled so badly.

It had been so real that he even imagined the sound of the blood dripping onto the floor. What an idiot he had been!

"Gotcha!" Alex jumped out of the bathroom, dressed in a blue robe, laughing so hard he could hardly breathe.

"Are you all right?" Niki asked, wide-eyed.

"He's fine!" said Terry in disgust. His voice was shaking again, but not from fear, from anger. "That was a rotten trick!" he told Alex. "We thought something had really happened to you!"

"I'm touched by your concern," said Alex with a pleased smirk. "Nice work, David."

"It did look pretty real," David said, also smirking.

"You mean you were in on it?" Terry asked David, furious.

"Sure he was," said Alex. "How else could we convince you wimps to waste all that time searching for my body? While you were running around trying to find the Silver Prince, the rest of the jock team finished the treasure hunt. Too bad, guys, you lose again!"

Niki turned to Alex, angry now herself. "That was really mean, Alex!" she said. "I never thought you could do something so rotten!"

For a moment Alex looked hurt, then he smirked again. "Hey," he said. "Don't you know all's fair in love and—Halloween tricks? Besides, Niki," he added, "I gave you plenty of chances to join the winning team."

"Come on, Terry," said Niki, grabbing his hand. "Let's go back to the party."

"Why don't you all clear out," said Alex. "I've got to change back into my costume—so my team can collect the prize for the treasure hunt."

As they walked back down to the living room, Terry's head was swimming. He liked surprises. But Alex's little trick had left him shaken.

I guess I still care about Alex, Terry thought. Otherwise I would have been able to think more clearly when I discovered that dummy in his costume hanging in the closet.

In the living room Murphy and Angela were dancing in the dim glow from the electric candles. The "treasures" were piled up on a table by the fireplace.

"Want some punch?" Terry asked Niki.

"Sounds great," she said. "I'll save you a seat. I need to talk to you."

Terry brought two cups of punch and then settled in the loveseat next to Niki. She was every bit as beautiful as she had been at the beginning of the evening, but her dark eyes were now narrowed with concern.

"Still upset about what Alex did?" Terry asked her.

"Not really," said Niki. "It's something else. Remember when I told you what I saw Justine saying the other day?"

Terry stopped her in surprise. "You don't still think she's up to something?" he said. "Justine's the only person at the party who hasn't done anything weird."

"Let me tell you what I found," Niki went on. "And tell me what you think. While you were on the treasure hunt, I went into Justine's room—"

"You were snooping in her room?"

"She didn't say any part of the house was off-limits," Niki reminded him. "Besides, I was curious. Terry, she doesn't have any of the normal high school stuff in her room—"

"Well, why should she?" said Terry. "She only moved here a few months ago. Besides, she's lived all over the world. She's probably more interested in stuff she got in her travels than pennants or school colors."

"She doesn't have things from her travels either," said Niki. "Her room is practically bare, except for one thing—"

She told Terry about the hidden closet and the clothes she'd found there, along with the picture of Justine and the older man.

"Right," said Terry. "Well, there's a simple explanation. Justine's a CIA agent and the guy's a Russian spy."

"Will you be serious!" said Niki, but she was laughing too. "Look, I know it sounds crazy, but nothing I found in Justine's room makes any sense. And I also found some prescription bottles made out to Enid Cameron."

"That's her CIA name," said Terry. "And that's why she's having the party. She's going to ask everyone on the guest list to be a spy."

"Maybe you're not so far off," said Niki. "Terry, I really think Justine leads some kind of double life."

"Well, maybe she does," said Terry. "But so what? If you're really that bugged about it, ask her. She's a very nice girl, and I'm sure she wouldn't want anybody to be suspicious of—"

He broke off as Justine rang her bell again. The dinging came from overhead, and all eyes turned to see Justine standing at the railing on the balcony above the living room, a gold foil-covered box on a table next to her.

"It's time to award the prize for the treasure hunt," she said. "And I'm so happy it was such a success. Even if"—she paused and smiled mischievously—"there was a surprise or two even *I* hadn't planned on."

Most of the kids applauded and cheered, and Justine made a small bow. "The prize is special chocolates from Paris," she said. "Who would like to accept them for the winning team?"

"I will," said Alex. He was back in costume, and handsome as ever as he slowly walked up the stairs to meet Justine.

"Perfect," she said breathily. "Golden chocolates—for a Silver Prince." She bent down to pick up the gold box, then staggered slightly and caught herself against the banister. Before she could hand the chocolates to Alex, the railing suddenly gave way—and with a bloodcurdling scream, Justine fell forward and plunged to the floor below!

chapter

10

She fell so fast, no one could move.

Her scream echoed off the high ceiling.

She landed hard on one of the dark crushed-velvet sofas beneath the balcony and didn't move.

Terry and the others ran to the sofa, too scared to speak.

Justine lay across the sofa, her eyes closed, her arm hooked crookedly over the sofa back.

Alex reached her before anyone else. "Justine!" he cried.

Her eyes opened and she slowly sat up.

"What happened?" she murmured, dazed.

Terry realized he'd been holding his breath. What can possibly happen next? he wondered.

"You fell," Alex told Justine gently. "Are you all right?"

"I think so," said Justine. "But how—"

"The banister—it just gave way," Alex said.

"But how could it?" said Justine. "It's solid—we had all the woodwork checked when we moved in here." She leaned against the cushion and gave a little gasp of pain. "My wrist—" she said.

"It may be sprained," said Alex, taking it in his hands. "Do you have an elastic bandage?"

While Trisha and Angela went for the bandage, the other kids started to climb the stairs to inspect the place where the banister had broken. But Philip was already up there, and despite his sad clown's mask he looked furious.

"All right!" he said in a stronger voice than Terry had heard him use all evening. It stopped everyone cold. "Which one of you kids did this?"

"Did what?" asked Murphy. "The banister just—"

"It was sawed!" said Philip.

He held up one end of the broken railing, and everyone could see that it had been cleanly cut through.

"The jocks did it!" Ricky blurted out, backing down the stairs with everyone else. "We heard some of their tricks were going to be dangerous!"

"We didn't do anything!" snarled Murphy. "Admit it was you guys—because you can't stand to lose!"

"Are you totally crazy?" protested Les. "Why would we do such a stupid thing? In fact, why would anyone?"

"I can think of a reason," said Alex, his face grim.

"Oh, yeah?" said Les. "What?"

"To make our team look bad," he said, staring directly at Terry.

"Are you accusing me of something?" Terry asked. "If so, say so."

"I'm not accusing anyone of anything," said Alex. "I just think it's funny that right after your team loses the treasure hunt, something bad happens."

"That's ridiculous!" said Terry. "When would we have had the time and privacy to do it? You're probably just covering up for doing it yourself! Isn't it enough that you had to cheat to win the treasure hunt? Do you want to kill someone too?"

Alex came down the last two stairs fast, breathing hard. "If you weren't an old friend," he said, "I'd—"

"Yeah?" said Terry, angry at himself for letting this dispute happen, but unable to back down. "You'd what?"

"Nothing," muttered Alex, deciding he'd be the one to let things chill out.

"Stop it! Can't you two stop it?" Niki was standing between them and shouting at both of them. "Something terrible has happened and all you two can do is fight about it!" She turned to Philip. "Mr. Cameron," she said, "we all feel terrible about this. But I'm sure no one here could have done such a terrible thing."

"Someone cut the banister," said Philip, downstairs now, sitting beside his niece. "And nearly killed my niece."

"Now, Uncle Philip," Justine said placatingly. "Whoever it was couldn't have known I'd be the one to lean on the railing—" She put an arm around her uncle's shoulders. "I just feel so bad that it's spoiled the party. All I ever wanted was for everyone to have a good time."

Philip stood and stepped away, shaking his head.

"Hey, no problem." Alex was at her side on the couch and slipped his arm around her. "Nothing's spoiled. It's a great party."

"Honest," chimed in Angela, wrapping Justine's wrist. "None of the things that have gone wrong are your fault. We're all having a good time."

"Really?" Justine asked in a tiny voice. "Thank you for saying so."

Now everyone else crowded around Justine, telling her what a great party it was. Justine turned her smile back on in full force.

"Thank you all so much," she said. "Maybe we just need a few minutes to catch our breath and relax, and then we'll get on with the party. After all, there are still plenty more surprises." She paused and stood up, then glanced around. "I'm going upstairs for a few minutes to get myself together. I'll see you guys soon."

"Whatever you say," Alex said. He had rested one hand lightly on the back of her neck and was looking at her as if no one else in the room existed. Justine whispered something in Alex's ear. Alex laughed and whispered something back. Then Justine headed upstairs.

How can Justine be with Alex? Terry wondered. Alex was probably the one who cut the banister, or at least knew who did.

"Those two are headed for nothing but trouble," Niki suddenly said. He saw that she, too, was watching Alex and Justine.

"I know what you mean," he agreed. "Someone ought to warn her."

"Warn *her?*" Niki's eyes flashed. "Someone ought to warn *him.* You may think I'm wrong, but I just don't trust her."

"You just have some kind of silly hunch, that's all," Terry said, surprised at how much he felt like defending Justine. "You know what, Niki, you're acting like you're—" He stopped himself before he said something he'd regret.

"I'm acting like I'm what?" Niki put a hand on Terry's cheek and pulled his face toward her. Her eyes were blazing—with anger and something else.

"Like you're—well—jealous!" Terry let it out. "Now that Alex is paying more attention to Justine than to you, you seem to think Justine is the Wicked Witch of the West."

For a moment Niki didn't answer. Her face had gotten very pale. "Is that what you really think?" she said at last.

"Look, I know you don't really care about Alex," said Terry. "But how come you're so down on Justine all of a sudden?"

"In the first place, I *do* care about Alex," Niki said. "As a friend. And I don't want to see him get hurt. In the second place, there's something about Justine that just isn't right. And if she didn't have you on her string, you'd see it yourself. Some very strange things have been happening—"

"Oh, right," said Terry, stung. "And I suppose you think Justine cut through the banister herself."

"I didn't say that," said Niki. "I don't know who cut through it. But that doesn't change the fact that Justine is playing some kind of game with all of us, and especially Alex."

"So now you're going to protect Alex?" Terry couldn't help saying it, even though he knew it would make things worse.

"What I'm going to do," said Niki, her voice cold with anger, "is find out what's going on. While there's still time!"

She turned abruptly and walked away.

Terry watched her go. Justine had a wide-screen TV set up and *Bride of Frankenstein* was on. Terry had never seen it, so he watched for a while. He was actually getting caught up in it when a deafening thunderclap rattled the house.

A moment later the screen went black and all the lights went out.

chapter
11

A few kids gasped.

Terry heard nervous laughter.

The glow from the fireplace provided the only light. The flickering flames sent eerie shadows playing across the walls.

Justine's voice cut through the darkness.

"You probably wonder if this is another of my surprises," she said with a little laugh. "But this surprise thunderstorm was provided by Mother Nature. And the dark is just perfect for the next game— if you're brave enough to play."

"Let's *par-tee!*" yelled Ricky.

"Sit down, Schorr!" someone yelled.

Terry squinted at his watch in the firelight and saw that it read three o'clock. There had been so much excitement, the time had gone quickly. He was surprised to realize that in just a few hours the party would be over.

He tried to see where Niki was. He knew she was somewhere in the shadows, but decided not to push it. She'd come back when she got over being mad.

Justine had begun to describe the new game, which she called Truth. "The idea is that you tell everyone the worst thing you've ever done," she explained. "Then everyone votes on whether you told the truth or not. If they think you were lying, you have to pay a penalty."

"That's the dumbest thing I ever heard," protested Murphy.

"Do you mean you're afraid to tell the truth in front of your friends?" Justine said.

"No way. I just think it's kinda dumb," he said, backing down. "But I'm not afraid."

"Good," said Justine before he could go on. "You see, the whole point of the game is for us to really get to know each other. Now who would like to go first?"

No one volunteered. Finally Justine turned her smile on Ricky. "Ricky, what about you?" she said. "Tell us what's the worst thing you ever did."

Ricky stood in front of the fireplace, obviously nervous and embarrassed. "I can't really talk about it," Ricky said uncomfortably.

"Hey, Schorr—that's not like you!" someone yelled. "Since when won't you talk about yourself?"

Everyone laughed.

Everyone but Ricky.

"Something really bad happened once," Ricky said, muttering to the floor. "On Fear Island. During an overnight with some kids. We thought someone was dead, and—" He stopped. "I really can't talk about it."

"Heavy!" someone shouted.

Someone else booed, unhappy that he wasn't going to hear the whole story.

"You have to be penalized for not telling the story," Justine said. "Your penalty is to stand on one foot until I say you can stop."

"On one foot?" protested Ricky. "I can never keep my balance."

"Then it's a perfect penalty," said Justine. "Okay, who's next—how about Angela?"

"The worst thing I ever did?" said Angela, standing and smiling. "That's easy. I stole my sister's boyfriend last summer. I called him up pretending I was her and got him to meet me. I let him know how much I liked him. I was sorry later though," she added. "He turned out to be a real loser."

Everyone laughed and applauded. When Angela sat down, Murphy got up and started telling something about cheating on a math test so he could keep his sports eligibility.

Terry thought the game was really stupid, and even a little cruel. He was sure Niki hated it too. Maybe the two of them could go off together and just talk.

He looked around, trying to spot her, and suddenly realized she wasn't anywhere in the living room.

Puzzled, he got up and checked the hall and kitchen, but there was no sign of Niki. With a sinking feeling he remembered that she had said she was going to find out what was going on.

When he returned to the living room, Ricky was still standing on one foot. "Can I stop now?" he begged Justine.

"If you're willing to tell us the truth about the worst thing you've ever done," she said.

"But I told the truth. It's just—other kids were

involved. It wouldn't be right for me to tell the story. And believe me, it's a real downer. It would bring everyone down." He looked very uncomfortable, and Terry felt sorry for him.

"Oh, all right, sit down," said Justine. Her fingers were intertwined with Alex's, and she leaned her head against his chest for a moment. "Who's next?" she said.

"How about *you?*" said Ricky.

"Oh, no," Justine replied with her mischievous smile. "I'm the hostess, so I get to go last. How about—Terry?" she said, spotting him.

"Uh, not right now," said Terry. "I'm, uh, looking for Niki. Has anyone seen her?"

"Not lately," said Trisha. "But it's so dark in here."

"Maybe she's hiding," said Murphy.

"Come to think of it," said Alex, "I haven't seen Les for a while either. Maybe she decided to switch wimps."

"Or maybe you know where she is!" said Terry.

"Give me a break," said Alex. "If you can't keep track of your own girlfriend, it's not my fault."

Terry had an angry reply ready, but before he could say anything, Justine stood up. "Will you two stop arguing?" she said. "You're spoiling the game."

Alex continued to glare at Terry. Terry glared back, then shrugged. "I'm going to find Niki," he announced to no one in particular.

He took a flashlight from the mantel and began to climb the stairs. It was still raining hard, but he could hear Alex and Murphy laughing in the living room.

"Looks like Terry's going on his own treasure hunt," said Murphy.

"Maybe he just can't face the truth," added Alex.

One by one Terry examined the rooms on the second floor. By the time he'd gotten to the last one, Justine's bedroom, he was beginning to feel a little nervous. Had he somehow missed Niki? Could she have—somehow—decided to go home?

He stood in the hall a moment, shining the flashlight its full length. At the far end rain splattered against a window, causing the glass to rattle and shake. Outside, flashes of lightning illuminated the whipping trees. For a moment he thought he heard the roar of motorcycles and froze, but then realized it was just thunder.

Niki wouldn't have gone home in such a storm, he realized. So she had to be somewhere in the house.

His eye fell on the stairs to the attic, and reluctantly, remembering what had happened the last time he went up there, he climbed the narrow staircase.

He shone the flashlight around the dusty room, illuminating piles of boxes. The lightning made their shadows seem to dance and jump, and the wind caused the whole room to creak, as if it were alive. In spite of himself, Terry felt cold dread move through his body.

Stop it, Terry, he told himself. You're letting your imagination play tricks because of what you found up here last time. This house is not haunted and there's nothing to be afraid of.

Maybe Niki is even back downstairs by now, he thought. He turned to leave, but then his eye fell on the closed closet door where he'd found the Silver Prince.

No.

There's no reason for Niki to be in there, he thought.

The feeling of dread became stronger.

This is ridiculous, he told himself. It's just a closet.

He reached out and slowly pulled the door open.

And froze in shock.

There, crumpled in a half-sitting position, was a body.

It had the handle of a large carving knife sticking out of its chest.

But this was no dummy, as the Silver Prince had been.

In the flashlight's beam there was no mistaking the staring, lifeless blue eyes behind the thick black-rimmed glasses.

It was Les Whittle.

chapter

12

"Very funny, Les," Terry said out loud, hoping he was wrong.

He reached out and touched him.

Les felt warm.

"All right, Les," he said. "Cut it out. It's me. Terry. We're on the same team, remember?"

Les didn't answer. He lay there, staring, not blinking, his eyes like marbles.

"A pulse," Terry said. "Where is your pulse, Les?"

He felt Les's wrist, then at the base of his throat. There was no movement.

He put his fingers in front of Les's mouth, but there was no breath.

Now Terry stared hard at Les's chest, trying not to think about the knife handle protruding from it. No movement. None at all.

No, Terry said to himself. No. No no no no no no no!

This can't be real.

It's another joke, another surprise. It's got to be.

"Don't be dead, Les," he said. "Please don't be dead."

But Les didn't answer. His unblinking eyes continued to stare out of his pale, pale face like the eyes of a department-store mannequin.

Scarcely able to stand, Terry backed out of the closet. His heart was beating so hard he could hear its pounding in his ears.

Shaking, he made his way back downstairs. His legs felt weak and rubbery as if he were trying to walk underwater. Or in a dream.

Please let it be a dream, he thought.

He had nearly reached the living room when a light shone in his face. It was David, just coming out of the bathroom.

"Hey, Terry," David said with surprise. "What happened to you? You look like you've seen a—"

"Les is dead," Terry said dully.

"What?"

"It's true. I just found him. In the closet. Upstairs."

"Hey, you're serious, aren't you?" said David. Terry couldn't think of an answer, but then David's eyes narrowed in suspicion. "Hey, wait a minute," he said. "You're trying to get back at me for the Silver Prince trick, aren't you?"

"Les is dead," Terry repeated. "He has a knife in his chest."

"And you're going to show it to me, right?" said David. "And then Les will jump up and yell gotcha!"

"He's never going to yell anything again," Terry said. He could feel himself starting to come out of the shock. "I don't care if you don't believe me. I've got to phone for help."

"Wait a minute," said David. "Let's go back upstairs. Maybe what you saw was another trick."

"No," said Terry.

"Sure?" said David. "Remember how real Alex looked? You were sure that was real too."

"I don't think it's a trick," said Terry. But he felt a little flicker of hope for the first time.

He went back up the stairs with David. As they started the last flight to the attic, Terry forced himself to be calm. I don't want to see Les's body again, he thought. But maybe David's right. Maybe I saw something and just thought it was Les.

His hand was still shaking as he reached out to open the closet door.

The closet was empty.

"I *knew* it!" said David. "This was just a trick to get me up here, right? What's next—a pie in the face?"

Terry just stared at the empty closet, relief flooding through him like a dam breaking.

It hadn't been real. Maybe he was going crazy. But having hallucinations was better than Les being dead.

"Terry?" Now David sounded concerned. "You all right?"

"He was here," Terry said. "Exactly the way I described it. I guess I must have somehow been—"

He stopped talking as his flashlight beam picked something up on the bottom of the closet.

"What is it?" asked David. And then he saw it too.

A thick, dark puddle on the closet floor.

Trembling, Terry reached down to touch it. His hand came away wet and sticky—and red.

"There's more," David said. Now his voice was shaking too.

Leading from the closet were drops and smears of blood.

Without a word, the boys followed the trail around the piles of boxes in the attic. Followed it to a window in the back.

The window was open, and rain slanted in, soaking the worn floorboards. A single smear of blood streaked the wall below the windowsill.

Terry didn't believe his heart could pound so loud and so fast. What had happened to Les's body? Had he—it—gotten up from the closet and escaped through the window?

Had Les somehow joined the Undead in the Fear Street woods?

"I'm going to look outside," David said. He sounded even more frightened than Terry felt.

Slowly David pushed the window the rest of the way open and stuck his head out into the rain. Terry crowded next to him.

They spotted it at the same time.

There, directly below them, on the peaked roof of a second-story dormer, lay Les's crumpled body, the knife glinting in the lightning.

chapter
———————
13

"We've got to get him," David said.

Terry couldn't think why, but he was glad to have something to do.

"One of us will have to go down there," said David. He found a piece of rope on the floor and began unwinding it.

"I'll go," said Terry, without thinking. He climbed onto the slippery windowsill, then dropped onto the shingles of the dormer below. The wind stung his face, and the rain was blowing so hard he could scarcely see.

He slipped and nearly fell, but caught the edge of the roof and steadied himself. "Hold on, Les," he said. "I'm coming."

David dropped the rope from the window. Terry caught the free end, then began to inch toward where Les lay.

The knife still stuck out from his chest, like some

strange sort of growth, and for the first time Terry realized not only that Les was dead, but that someone had killed him.

Murdered him.

Someone at the party was a murderer.

Terry forced himself to put that thought out of his mind and concentrated on crossing the sloping shingles. One step at a time, he told himself.

Les's glasses had fallen off and his skin was no longer warm. But his eyes were still open, and Terry tried not to look at them as he tied the rope around Les, above where the knife was sticking out.

Then he pulled and dragged the body till it was just under the window and lifted while David pulled on the other end of the rope. Somehow, they got the body up over the windowsill and into the room. Then Terry boosted himself up through the window.

For a moment both boys just stared at their dead friend, both breathing hard. Finally David shut the window. "We've got to cover him up with something," he said.

Terry nodded. They searched in the dusty attic till they found an old blanket. They straightened Les's body, then covered him.

Now that they had finished, Terry realized they had to face the next big hurdle—what to do next.

"We'd better call the police," he said.

David nodded. "Shouldn't we tell everyone what happened?"

Terry thought a moment. "Not till we talk to the police," he said. "After all—someone here is a murderer. We don't want him to get away."

"Let's talk to Philip at least," said David. "It might be better if he makes the call."

They went back to the living room as if nothing had happened. It seemed to Terry that hours had passed, but a glance at his watch told him it had only been a few minutes.

The other guests were still playing Truth. Alex was standing on his head in a corner of the room, and Terry guessed he was paying a penalty, but he didn't really care. All idea of fun and games was gone—for good.

"Hi, guys," Justine said cheerily. "Ready for Truth?"

"Not just yet," said Terry. "I need to ask your uncle something. Do you know where he is?"

"Isn't he in here?" said Justine. "Or the kitchen?"

"I haven't seen him," said Angela.

"Maybe he's disappeared too," said Murphy, laughing. "Like Niki and Les. Maybe there's a Bermuda triangle somewhere right in the middle of this house."

Niki!

After Terry had found Les's body, he'd forgotten all about her. She was still missing, and there was a murderer in the house.

All he could think of was to run back upstairs and start searching for her again. But David clapped a hand on his shoulder.

"Come on, Terry," he said, sounding almost normal. "Let's go see if Philip is in the kitchen."

Right, Terry told himself. Call for help. That's definitely the first thing to do.

He followed David into the kitchen. An open window was banging in the wind, and next to it hung a wall phone, slick with rain.

His fingers still trembling, Terry picked up the phone and started to punch in 911. But there was no dial tone. "The line's dead," he whispered, wondering what else could go wrong.

"Maybe the wind knocked the line loose," said David. "It was strong enough to blow open that window."

"Let me look," said Terry. He unlocked the back door and peered out. "The line comes in just above the window," he said. "Maybe it—"

"It's cut!" said David. He stepped out onto the porch, pointing. There was no question—the line hung in two pieces, obviously cut through.

The two boys exchanged glances. Terry wondered if he looked as scared as David did.

"Do you think the murderer did this?" Terry asked.

"It was Bobby and Marty," David said. "It had to be. Who else could it be?"

Terry thought it over. Could Marty and Bobby have killed Les?

"They could have sneaked back and come in the window," said David, obviously wondering the same thing.

No. Impossible, Terry thought.

The two bikers swaggered around a lot and pretended to be hard. But they weren't murderers.

Someone is, said a voice in his head.

Someone is a murderer. Someone you know.

Someone at this party.

The only thing he knew for sure was that they had to get help—as soon as possible. And that he couldn't leave the mansion until he found Niki.

"We've got to find Philip," David said. "Then one of us can go for help."

The boys ran back into the house and through the front hall. Terry glanced out a window panel beside the front door. Across the yard Marty's wrecked motorcycle glinted in the lightning like a warning signal of doom.

A particularly bright flash lit up the yard then, and something caught Terry's eye.

Quickly he ran out to the motorcycle, David close behind. Crumpled in the mud, just beneath the front wheel, was a blue satin jacket—Philip's clown costume.

Terry examined the jacket. One whole arm was stained with blood.

chapter
14

"This is a joke, right?" Murphy was saying. "It's another trick—"

"Sure it is," said Alex. "Terry's still mad that the wimps lost the treasure hunt, and this is his mature way of showing it. Did he pay you off to go along with it, Dave?"

"It's no joke!" said David, shaking slightly in his wet clothes. He and Terry were standing in front of the fireplace, drying off. They were facing the remaining party guests. Tentative smiles and laughs had turned to expressions of horror as they began to realize that this Halloween trick might be for real.

Trisha spoke now, trying to fight back tears. "Are you telling us that Les is—is dead?"

"Murdered," said Terry grimly.

"But who—?"

"And Uncle Philip?" Justine spoke for the first time. "Something has happened to him too?"

"We don't know for sure," said Terry. "But we found his jacket covered with blood."

Justine buried her face in her hands and began to cry. Alex, who had been sitting next to her, put one arm around her and patted her gently with the other.

Angela stood up, shaking. "Someone—someone in this house is a—a murderer!" she said. Her voice sounded very high-pitched and almost hysterical.

"Or someone *outside* the house," said David. He told the others about the cut phone line.

"I—I want to go home!" Angela said. "I have to get out of here!" She ran toward the front door, with Ricky and Murphy both after her.

"You can't go out!" said Ricky. "It's really pouring now!"

"Besides," Murphy added, "Marty and Bobby might still be out there!"

"I don't care!" she shrieked. She slipped away from them and rushed through the door. An instant later there was a cry from the front porch.

Murphy and Ricky rushed outside. A moment later Ricky came in, more frightened than ever. "It's okay," he said. "She fell down. She tripped on the piece of plywood Marty and Bobby put down as a ramp."

Murphy came inside carrying Angela. She was still crying but no longer sounded hysterical. "My ankle," she moaned.

"I think it's sprained," said Murphy. He set her down on one of the sofas.

"You'll have to carry me home, Murphy," Angela said. "I don't think I can walk."

"I'll help," said Alex.

"Stop!" Justine cried suddenly. "Don't leave me

alone! Please! Wait till morning! We can all go for help then!"

"We've got to call the police," said David gently. "But there's no reason for everyone to go. There's a pay phone at the corner of Fear Street and the Old Mill Road. It should only take me a few minutes to drive there."

Terry thought about the walk through the cemetery to get to the cars and wondered how David could face it. But he knew David was right—he had to go. In any case, Terry had to stay there to find Niki.

"Don't worry," said David. "You'll be safe here as long as you all stay together. Don't leave the living room and lock the front door. I'll be back with help in just a few minutes."

He pulled on his varsity jacket and slipped out the front door. For a moment the only sound in the room was Angela's muffled sniffling. Then Ricky got up and locked the front door.

Everyone had crowded closer together in front of the fire, and even Justine seemed lost and frightened in the flickering light.

"It'll only be a few minutes," said Trisha soothingly to Angela. "As long as we all stick—Terry, where are you going?"

"I still don't know where Niki is," he said, trying to sound calmer than he felt. "I was looking for her when I found Les."

"This isn't just a trick?" said Alex suspiciously.

"What do you think?" Terry snapped. "Do you see Niki anywhere? She's been missing for over an hour!"

"I'm sorry, man," said Alex, suddenly frightened. "I'll help you look for her."

For a moment Terry wanted to tell Alex to mind his

own business. But he read an expression of real concern on his former friend's face and realized for the first time how much Alex really cared for Niki. Besides, he told himself, the most important thing wasn't who found her, but to find her as quickly as possible.

And too much time had passed already.

With a growing sense of urgency, Terry realized that it might already be too late.

As he walked toward the woods surrounding the cemetery, David realized he had never been so scared in his life. He had volunteered to go for help because he couldn't stand the thought of just waiting in the mansion with Les's body there. But he couldn't get Les out of his mind.

Every time he closed his eyes he saw Les's staring, sightless face.

Every time the wind shook the trees he saw the skeleton costume.

The rain was slanting down harder than ever, and he was soaked completely through. His body had started to shiver from the cold, and from fear.

It was taking him a lot longer to get to the cemetery than he remembered. The ground was deeply rutted and now so slippery with mud that he had to watch every step. The wind had shifted and was blowing directly in his face, as if to force him back to the Cameron mansion.

The only good thing was that there'd been no sign of Bobby and Marty. Maybe the weather had gotten too bad for them.

The wall surrounding the Fear Street cemetery loomed just ahead. He pushed open the gate and began to pick his way along the path between the grave markers, trying not to think about where he was.

With every boom of thunder, lightning lit up the graveyard like a snapshot, the old gravestones standing out in eerie relief.

It was only a few more yards to the end of the graveyard and where the cars were parked. In a flash of lightning he finally saw them in the distance and felt a flood of relief for the first time in hours.

In just a few more steps he'd be out of there and on his way to help. At last he reached the gate, swung it open, and began to run toward the handful of cars parked at the end of Fear Street.

He reached into his pocket and took out his keys as he approached his red Corolla.

And stopped, holding them in his hand.

The Corolla was sitting at an odd angle. Every one of its tires had been slashed. Every tire on every car belonging to the guests had been slashed.

chapter
———
15

*B*obby and Marty, David thought.

He'd come all the way through the cemetery and now he wouldn't get any farther. What could he do now? Somehow, he had to get help. But it was a very long walk back to town.

A flash of lightning illuminated the houses along this end of Fear Street, and David realized he could simply go to one of them and ask to use the phone. Never mind that half the houses were abandoned and the other ones were supposed to be haunted, or that it was so late.

This was an emergency.

He stood looking at the nearest houses a moment, then set out for the closest one—and was stopped by the roar of a motorcycle.

Bobby and Marty, both on Bobby's motorcycle, came roaring out from behind the cemetery and stopped directly in his path.

"Going somewhere, David?" Bobby said.

"The party's in the other direction," added Marty. "We thought maybe you'd help us get back in."

"Especially when you see what'll happen if you don't," said Bobby.

Both boys' words were slurred, and David realized they'd been drinking heavily—probably since they had crashed the party earlier.

"Come on, David," said Marty nastily. "What do you say?"

Suddenly David had had enough. After everything that had happened, he wasn't going to let himself be pushed around by a couple of bullies. A nagging voice in the back of his mind reminded him that Marty and Bobby might be murderers, but he dismissed it. They were too cowardly to do anything really terrible, he thought. Besides, he was too angry to think straight.

"Get out of my way!" David said angrily, and took another step toward the house across the street.

Bobby revved his engine. "Hey, cool your jets, man," he said.

"David seems to have forgotten his manners," Marty said. He had pulled the heavy chain out of his jacket, and, holding it menacingly, stepped off the bike.

"I don't have time for this!" David said, furious. "Something terrible has happened!"

"Something even more terrible is *about* to happen," said Marty, taking a step toward him. "To you."

For the first time since Marty and Bobby had showed up, David began to be afraid of them. He realized they had been drinking too much to know what they were doing.

"All right, all right," David said, backing up. "Take it easy."

"Hey, what's the matter, man?" said Marty. "Don't feel so brave anymore?"

"Look," said David, searching desperately for a way to escape, "I don't have any problem with you guys. So why don't you just go away and leave me alone?"

"No can do," said Bobby, just behind Marty.

Both bikers were so intent on violence that David realized his only hope was to get away from them. He spun around and, slipping on the wet ground, dashed back into the graveyard.

Bobby and Marty were right behind him. They moved surprisingly quickly, considering how drunk they were.

David ran down a long path, a blur of tombstones flying by on either side of him. He was heading toward the wall and then the Fear Street woods.

"Ow!" He caught his foot on a root and went down in the mud.

He was just pulling himself to his feet when Bobby and Marty caught up to him.

"Hey, dude—wait up," said Bobby drunkenly.

"You shouldn't run away. It could be dangerous." Marty cocked his arm and took a swing at David's head. David easily ducked, but he slipped again and felt a sickening crack as his head hit the corner of a gravestone.

He saw a bright flash of light, and then everything went dim, as if someone had pulled a curtain down over his head.

Through the curtain, he could faintly hear Bobby's and Marty's voices. They seemed like figures in a faraway place.

"What'd you do?" said Bobby's voice, sounding frightened.

"Nothing!" said Marty. "He slipped and hit his head."

"He looks hurt bad," said Bobby. "What if he dies?"

"Then we don't want to be anywhere around here," said Marty. "Come on, let's move him out of sight."

David knew they were talking about him, but somehow the words didn't make any sense. He was very sleepy. He felt himself being dragged along the ground.

The light became dimmer and dimmer and then faded out completely.

chapter

16

Terry didn't really like the idea of Alex helping him find Niki, but he realized it made sense. Too much time had passed already.

Please, he thought. Please let her be okay.

"I've already checked on the second floor," he told Alex. "Why don't you check it again in case I've missed something."

"Wait," said Justine. "I'll go. I know the house better than anyone."

"I'll go with you," said Alex.

"No, Alex," she said sweetly. "You wait in the living room with the others—in case anything happens." Alex was about to protest again, but Justine leaned over and kissed him on the cheek. "Please—let me do this. I feel so terrible about everything that's happened. At least let me try to help Terry."

Grumbling, Alex went back to join the others by the fireplace.

"Thanks, Justine," Terry said. "Please be careful."

"I promise," she said. "Why don't you check down here while I go upstairs?"

Terry nodded. The only place he hadn't looked was the basement. He didn't really think Niki would have gone down there alone, but couldn't think of anywhere else to look.

As he started down the dark, narrow steps, he could hear the others talking in hushed, frightened tones back in the living room. Please, he kept thinking over and over. Please, please, please.

This was the first time he'd gone down to the basement. Each step creaked like something alive, and he wondered if the stairs were strong enough to hold him.

The flashlight showed thick ropes of cobwebs and splintered, dusty beams. It was obvious that Justine and her uncle hadn't done any renovations on this part of the house.

The basement itself was jammed full of old boxes and splintered boards. He jumped as something skittered across the floor behind him. It's just a mouse, he told himself. At least I hope it's a mouse.

Niki can't be down here, he thought. He wanted to call out her name, but knew she couldn't hear him even if she was there.

He heard another noise, a kind of thumping, from the far end of the low, dark space. In the circle of light he saw a large storage closet set against the wall. Gingerly, he approached it and yanked the door open.

Inside was what he first thought was a bundle of rags.

And then the bundle moved.

It was Niki.

She stared up at him with a dazed expression. "Terry?"

"Funny Face!" Terry dropped to his knees and put his arms around her. He held her tightly, overwhelmed with relief that she was alive. Finally he let her go and shone the flashlight so she could see his face.

"Are you all right?" he said.

"Where are we?" asked Niki, looking around in confusion.

"In the basement of Justine's house," said Terry. "In a closet."

"The *basement?*" said Niki. "How on earth did I get—"

"I don't know," said Terry. "What happened to you?"

"I'm not sure," she said. "I think someone knocked me out."

"Knocked you out!" Terry felt his heart begin to race. He searched Niki's face and saw that she had a large purple bruise on her forehead. "Tell me what you remember, Funny Face."

Niki pulled herself to her feet and brushed the dust off her red gown. She squinted, remembering. "Right after we had that—that silly argument," she said, "I went back up to Justine's room. It was really dark and spooky, but I kept thinking there had to be something I'd missed, something that would explain the strange way Justine's been acting.

"I went back in the secret closet," Niki went on, "and this time I noticed a shoe box on the floor. None of the other shoes were in boxes, so I opened it. It was full of mementos—old pictures, some pressed flowers, and—and this." She reached in her pocket and handed Terry a brittle news clipping from the Shadyside paper.

Terry took the clipping and shone the flashlight on it. In growing confusion and disbelief he began to read:

Local Couple Killed in Fiery Crash

Edmund D. Cameron, 26, and his wife, Cissy, 20, were killed late last night when their car was hit head-on by a car driven by James B. Whittle, 16.

The Camerons' car, a late-model Ford, was headed south on Old Mill Road when it was hit by Whittle's car, a Chevrolet station wagon. According to witnesses at the scene, Whittle had been drag racing with another car, a Corvette driven by John McCormick, 16. The Cameron car spun out of control and into a ditch, where it burst into flames.

"I didn't see anything till it was too late," Whittle said. "They just showed up in the fog. I feel terrible about it."

Whittle's car sustained major damage, while the Corvette was untouched. Neither Whittle nor McCormick, nor any of their passengers, was seriously injured. Those riding with Whittle included Evelyn Sayles, 15, Joanne Trumble, 15, Arlene Coren, 16, and Robert Carter, 14. The passengers in the Corvette were Jim Ryan, 18, Nancy Arlen, 16, and Ed Martiner, 15, all of Shadyside.

The Cameron couple are survived by a daughter, Enid, age 1.

No charges were filed pending police investigation.

Terry quickly finished reading the article. "This must be the accident that killed the original owners of the mansion!" he said. "What a horrible way to die—burning to death in a car!"

"Yes," agreed Niki. "No wonder it made Justine crazy."

"What are you talking about?" said Terry.

"Terry, the couple who were killed in that crash—they were Justine's parents!"

Terry just stared at her. "Maybe we ought to get you to a doctor," he said. "After all, someone hit you on the head—"

"Oh, for heaven's sake!" said Niki in exasperation. "Are you really so afraid to look at the truth?"

"But Justine's parents—Justine—it doesn't make any sense," Terry protested. "Besides, the clipping says their daughter was named Enid."

"Remember? That's the name I saw on those prescriptions," Niki said. "Besides, look at this." She reached in her pocket for something. It was a driver's license, showing Justine's picture and made out to Enid J. Cameron.

Terry looked at it, shocked. "Well," he said finally, "I guess Justine isn't a distant cousin after all. But why would she want us to think she's someone else?"

"You still don't understand, do you?" said Niki. "Did you notice the names of the people in the accident?"

Quickly Terry scanned the clipping again. "Whittle," he said. "McCormick. Sure, they're some of the same names as some of our friends. But so what? Shadyside is a small place."

"Terry, they're not just the same names as some of our friends—they're the names of our parents! Didn't you see your father's name? Jim Ryan?"

"I guess I just skimmed it," admitted Terry. "But what about the other names—Joanne Trumble, Arlene Coren—"

"Arlene is my mother," said Niki. "Coren is her maiden name."

Terry just stood a moment, thinking about what Niki had told him. He didn't want to think about what it might mean.

"There's another thing," Niki went on. "Did you see the date of the article?"

"Yeah, it's—let's see," said Terry, doing some quick mental arithmetic. "Twenty-eight years ago." And then he realized what that meant. "So Justine is—is—"

"Nearly thirty years old!" Niki finished for him. "Terry, she's not a high school student! She's a grown woman!"

"A double life," said Terry. He let out a low whistle. "I wonder what Justine would say if she knew you found this stuff."

"I think she already knows," Niki said. "Or somebody does. After I put away the shoe box I started back to tell you what I'd found. Only before I could close the secret door someone must have snuck up on me. I remember bending down to pull the door shut, and the next thing I knew I was in this closet." She touched her finger to the bruise on her head.

Terry leaned down and gently kissed the bruised spot.

"Thank heaven nothing worse happened to you," he murmured.

Niki looked carefully at his face. "What do you mean worse?" she said. "Terry, is there something you're not telling me?"

"Oh, Niki," he said. He squeezed her hand, hard. "So much has been happening." Quickly he told her about finding Les's body and Philip's bloodstained jacket. When he finished, Niki was paler than ever. "So you can imagine," he said, "how worried I was. I thought that maybe you had been—had been . . ."

"I can't imagine why she let me go," Niki said. "She just must not have had the time to—to do with me what she did to Les."

"She?" said Terry. "You think Justine killed Les?"

"Who else could it be?" said Niki. "Terry, look at the facts! First, there was the invitation list—"

"Okay," he said, thinking. "So Justine invited us—the children of the kids who were in that crash—"

"That's right," said Niki. "And *only* us. Didn't you think it was strange that she insisted no one else could even come to the party, not even as a date?"

"Yeah, I see what you mean," said Terry. "I guess I'm still having a hard time believing it."

"That's why she's getting away with it!" said Niki. "Because no one would believe that sweet, innocent Justine could be a murderer. But, Terry, we have to face it. Justine had us here to this party for one reason only."

She paused, then went on, her voice suddenly shaking. "For revenge!"

chapter

17

"Niki," Terry said, "we've got to get back upstairs quick! David went to get help. So if Justine's planning anything else, she'll do it soon, before the police get here!"

Without another word, Terry and Niki raced up the basement stairs and back into the living room. Everyone was sitting as Terry had left them, huddled close to the fireplace, looking scared and miserable.

Everyone but Justine. She was sitting on the edge of one of the chairs, a strange look of excitement on her face. When she saw Terry and Niki she smiled her most open, friendly smile.

"Oh, good!" she said as if nothing had happened. "You found Niki. Now we can get on with the rest of the party."

"Get on with the party!" Terry said, flabbergasted. "How can you even think of such a thing! Justine, we know the truth! We know you murdered Les!"

For the next few seconds no one could hear anything, because everyone was talking at once.

"Have you guys been drinking?" Murphy demanded.

"I know what this is," said Alex. "It's the last try of the wimps to scare the rest of us away. But it won't work, Terry. Forget it."

"Listen to me!" Niki shouted. "I have a newspaper clipping! It proves—"

But before she could reach for the clipping, Justine suddenly started laughing and clapping her hands. Everyone turned and stared at her.

"Perfect!" she said. "Niki, Terry, you both are perfect! You're even better than when we rehearsed it. If I weren't in on it, *I'd* even believe you thought I was a murderer."

"You mean," gasped Trisha, "that this really is just another—"

"It's another surprise," said Justine. "The next to last one of the evening. And I'm sorry if it frightened some of you, but what's Halloween without a good scare?"

"She's lying!" Niki shouted. "Don't listen to her!"

"This isn't a trick!" Terry added. "Trisha, Alex, all of you, listen to us! Think about what's happened!"

"What about Les?" Trisha suddenly asked suspiciously.

"What about him?" said Justine. "He was in on it too."

"Come off it, Justine," Terry said. "Les is dead. I saw his body. And you killed him."

Justine laughed again, as if this were the best joke she had ever heard. "You can stop now, Terry," she said. "I think everyone has gotten the point."

"You're denying you killed him?" said Terry.

"If I killed Les," Justine said, wiping tears of laughter from her face, "how come he and I were just having a good laugh upstairs?"

"But—" said Terry.

"Justine," said Niki at the same time, "I saw your—"

Justine cut them both off. "Come on, guys, lighten up! Forget about Les, and let's move on—to the last surprise of the night."

chapter

18

"*I* can't believe you did this!" Murphy grumbled. "Even worse, I can't believe we fell for it!"

"Does this mean the wimp team wins?" asked Ricky.

"No way," said Alex. "Besides, you had help from Justine." Like all the others, he was obviously relieved.

Terry couldn't believe his friends could be so blind. "Come on, Ricky—this is for real!" he cried.

He glanced at Niki, who was shaking with rage and frustration. "This is nuts! They all believe Justine," she whispered. "We've *got* to convince them we're all in terrible danger!"

"I don't think we can," Terry said. "But you and I know the truth. Why don't we get out of here while there's still time?"

Niki shook her head. "We can't do that, Terry," she said. "We can't leave them alone with her. Not when they trust her. We'll just have to hope that David gets here soon with help."

Terry knew she was right.

"Justine," said Niki sweetly, "if this is all just a trick, then where is your uncle Philip?"

"Don't you remember?" Justine said, sounding exasperated. "He went out for more sodas."

That was the dumbest answer Terry could imagine, but the others didn't seem to notice. Terry decided to try another tack. "You told us you and Les were just talking," he said. "But nobody has seen him. If this was all just a trick, where is he?"

"I thought you'd never ask," said Justine, hopping up from where she was sitting. "Les is in the dining room, helping me prepare the final surprise."

Everyone started to move toward the dining room, but Justine raised her hand. "Wait just a minute," she said. "I want to make sure everything is perfect." She turned and went into the dining room, leaving the door slightly open.

"Our trick worked perfectly, Les!" everyone heard her say. "Thanks for all your help."

From the other side of the door, Terry and the others heard Justine continue to chat with Les. Terry felt the hair on the back of his neck prickle.

Then Justine reappeared at the door. "Come on, everybody," she said. "Everything's ready for you now."

Everyone hurried into the dining room, with Ricky and Murphy supporting Angela as she hopped on one foot. In the center of the room was a long, polished table, with a big candelabrum in the middle. Around the table were small gift-wrapped boxes at each place.

And at the head of the table sat Les.

He was wearing big, oval-shaped sunglasses that reflected the candles' glow.

"Find your places," Justine said. "Each box has a name on it."

But no one paid any attention to the gift boxes. Instead they all crowded around Les.

Murphy balled up his fist and half jokingly held it in Les's face. "Hey, man, you scared us silly!" he said. "We were actually worried about you."

"Yeah," Alex agreed. "I never thought I'd be glad to see *you!*"

Les didn't answer.

"It was a good trick, Les," said Trisha. "But it wasn't fair to pull it on your own team. Why didn't you say something?"

Les didn't answer.

Terry looked at him more closely. Something wasn't right. Les wasn't moving. Not at all. Terry touched his friend on the shoulder, and Les slowly toppled off the chair onto the floor. The dark glasses flew off, revealing his staring, and very dead, eyes.

"He's dead," Terry said, feeling cold all over. "I knew it."

Someone screamed.

"I think I'm going to be sick," Trisha said.

Terry turned quickly, just in time to see Justine dart outside, slamming the door behind her.

An instant later a key turned.

Terry knew without looking. They were locked in.

chapter

19

The only window was covered with a heavy metal security grate, and there was only one door.

Murphy immediately began pounding on it, but it was solid oak. "Let us out!" he shouted.

Alex and Ricky pulled and pried at the security grate, but it wouldn't budge.

"We're trapped!" Angela yelled shrilly. "She's trapped us in here with a—a—dead—"

"Calm down, Angela," said Niki, taking her gently by her shoulders.

"Yes," agreed Trisha, her own voice shaking. "We've got to keep calm—we've got to think clearly. . . ."

At that moment Justine's little bell rang, from outside the window. "Surprise!" she called in to them, her face close to the security grate. She was shining a powerful flashlight on her face. They hurried to the window. It had stopped raining, they saw.

"Now, wasn't this the best Halloween trick of all?" Justine said, obviously pleased with herself.

"Let us out of here, Justine," said Terry. "I don't know what you have in mind, but David will be back any minute—with the police!"

"Then I'd better hurry, hadn't I?" she said calmly. She smiled at all her guests, a cruel, mocking smile. "It's time for the last surprise of the evening," she said. "But first I want you all to sit at your places at the table and open the gift boxes."

"You've lied to us from the beginning!" said Alex. "Why should we do anything you say?"

"Because," said Justine coldly, "I will be very angry if you spoil my surprise. And who knows what I might do then? Now, find your places!"

One by one the guests drifted to the table and sat down. For a minute or so the only sound was of chairs scraping along the floor, punctuated by sniffling from Angela.

"Is everybody ready?" said Justine. "Good. Now we will finish playing Truth. Only this time it's my turn to tell the truth—and for you to pay the penalty."

She smiled her crazy smile, and Terry again felt cold. Maybe she just wanted to talk, he hoped. He'd heard that some insane people simply needed a chance to talk about the things that were bothering them. Besides, she was outside the house—what could she possibly do to them in there?

"Before I begin," Justine went on, "I'd like you to unwrap your packages." She waited while the guests untied the boxes. Inside each one was an identical photograph of a smiling young couple dressed in clothes of the sixties. The woman had dark hair, but she looked hauntingly like Justine.

"The pictures are of a couple named Edmund and Cissy," Justine told them. "Now I want you to look at the pictures while I tell you a story." She glanced around the room to make sure everyone was looking at a copy of the picture. "Edmund and Cissy," Justine began, "were just like you—young, full of happiness and hope for the future. They were full of hope, that is, until twenty-eight years ago tonight." She paused, then went on in a singsong way, as if she had memorized a script.

"Twenty-eight years ago it was Halloween, just like tonight. Edmund and Cissy had been visiting friends. They were on their way home to their one-year-old daughter, whom they loved very much. Their car was going south on Old Mill Road."

Again she paused. Even though he knew what was coming, Terry couldn't help listening, fascinated, as the story unfolded.

"At the same time," Justine continued, "there were two cars full of teenagers driving north on Old Mill Road. They had just been to a Halloween party and were still partying. They decided to drag. There were exactly nine of them in the two cars.

"One block from the corner of Fear Street and Old Mill Road, one of the cars with teenagers in it collided head-on with the car carrying the young couple. Their car rolled into a ditch and burst into flames. By the time firemen got there, it was too late to save them."

Terry could tell from the looks on the other guests' faces that most of them had guessed the truth by now.

Angela and Trisha were both crying, tears running down their faces.

Justine went on, her face cruel and old looking in the flashlight beam. "I want you to shut your eyes now and imagine what Edmund and Cissy felt that night," she said. "Imagine how it felt to be trapped in a burning car, the heat unbearable, with no possible escape. And no one to help you no matter how loudly you screamed. You may have guessed by now that Edmund and Cissy were my parents. But you may not have guessed the names of the teenagers in the other two cars." She recited names slowly. Terry heard gasps as different guests recognized the names of their own parents.

"None of the teenagers were even hurt," Justine said. "None of them ever paid for what they did to my parents. So I have decided that you, their children, will pay."

There wasn't a sound from the dining room, except for the sniffling of Angela and Tricia.

"Les had the honor of paying first," said Justine, "because it was his father who drove the car that killed my parents. The rest of you will go together, the way your parents should have all those years ago."

"No!" Angela screamed suddenly. "How can you make us responsible for something that happened before we were born? It's not fair!"

"What happened to my parents wasn't fair either!" cried Justine.

"Let us go," Murphy pleaded. "We won't tell anyone what we know!"

Justine scrutinized him a moment, then burst into laughter. "Do you really think it's that easy?" she said.

Terry looked at Niki, feeling hopeless. He didn't know what Justine had in mind, but he was sure it was something horrible.

"We've got to keep her talking," Niki whispered.

"What?"

"As long as Justine is talking, she can't do anything to us," Niki said. "So we've got to stall her until the police come."

If they come, Terry thought. David had been gone for quite a while. Still, Niki's idea made sense. "Justine—" he called. She turned to him, annoyed.

"What is it now?" she said.

"I just—I just wanted to know how you managed to fool all of us so completely. I mean—everything seems to be planned down to the last detail."

Justine was obviously pleased. "I'm glad you appreciate my efforts," she said. "I've been planning this for a very long time. And I must admit—even I didn't suspect how successful it would be."

"So all of it—the invitations, the surprises—all were part of your plan?"

"Of course," said Justine. "Everything was leading up to this moment. And now it's time—"

Niki interrupted her again. "But how could you do it all?" she said. "For instance, someone hit me and carried me downstairs. It couldn't have been you—"

"But of course it was!" Justine smiled just exactly as if someone had complimented her on her hair.

"But how did you get me down to the basement?" Niki went on. "I know you're strong, but even you couldn't carry me that far."

"I didn't have to," said Justine smugly. "There's an old dumbwaiter system in the house. I just put you into it on the second floor and then lowered you to the basement."

"What about the cut banister?" said Terry. "Did you do that too?"

Justine laughed. "What do you think?" she said. "I realized before the party that someone might suspect me, so I arranged for my little accident. It wasn't hard at all. When I was a teenager, I studied gymnastics."

She's thought of everything, Terry thought. We don't have a chance. He tried to come up with something else to ask Justine, to keep her talking, but his mind had gone blank.

"What about Les?" said Niki suddenly.

"What *about* him?" said Justine.

"The others heard you talking to him before we came in here," Niki said.

Justine laughed, a scornful laugh. "They heard me. But I'd be willing to bet they didn't hear Les's side of the conversation! But time is wasting," Justine said, her smile fading. "If you will look up toward the ceiling, you will see that I have put up some state-of-the-art speakers for your entertainment."

Terry glanced up, surprised. As Justine had said, four huge speakers were attached high on the walls just below the ceiling.

"The speakers are connected to a battery-powered cassette deck I have out here," Justine went on. "Which reminds me. It's time to begin your penalty."

"But what about—" said Terry.

"No," said Justine. "No more questions. It's time to get on with the rest of the surprise." Again she smiled, a smile so sweet that it was shocking in contrast with the terrible things she was saying.

"When I started thinking about how to make you pay," she said, "I realized that I wanted you to suffer the same way my parents had suffered long ago. But I couldn't arrange a car accident. And then I realized I could easily reproduce the worst parts of a car wreck." She ducked below the window a moment, then stood up again. "I just switched on a tape that I made especially for you," she said.

A low rumbling began to come from the huge speakers. Terry recognized the sound of a car engine starting up.

"Since I can't re-create a real accident," Justine went on, "I'm going to make you *hear* what it is like, hear the shriek of twisting metal, the screams of pain from the terrified victims . . ."

The sound of the engine grew louder, and now there were new sounds, those of tires squealing around curves as the taped car picked up speed.

Is this what she's going to do to us? Terry wondered in shock. Make us listen to a tape of car crashes? Is that all?

"Of course, just hearing the sounds of an accident isn't enough," Justine went on as if she'd read his thoughts. "For you to really pay, you must also experience the pain they experienced, and die the way they died." She flicked on a cigarette lighter.

"I've piled a bunch of oily rags in the area just outside the dining room," she said. "I'm going to go in and light them now. It will take a few minutes for the flames to reach you. You'll have plenty of time to think about what my parents suffered—and what's going to happen to you!"

She bent down again, then walked away from the window. Terry wanted to talk to the others, to try to plan an escape, but the soundtrack on the tape quickly grew from loud to deafening. He couldn't hear anything as the car on the tape speeded up.

A moment later there was a sickening squeal of brakes, the crunch of twisting metal, shattering glass, and then the screams—screams of pain—and terror. Over and over these sounds played, so loud that Terry could feel their vibrations in his whole body.

To the screams on the tape were added the screams of the guests trapped in the dining room, their hands clapped over their ears as they tried to shut out those dreadful, overwhelming noises. It was the most horrifying experience Terry had ever been through. He didn't think anything could be worse.

And then the first tendrils of smoke began to seep under the dining-room door.

chapter

20

*I*t was like a scene from a nightmare, Niki
thought as she watched her friends scream and writhe,
trying to blot out the terrible sounds. Even Terry had
his eyes squeezed shut, his hands pressed tightly to his
ears.

When the smoke began to filter into the room, the
hysteria grew even greater. Alex and Murphy began
beating on the window bars, clawing at them. Both
boys had blood all over their hands and running down
their arms, but they didn't seem to notice.

Niki could feel the vibrations from the tape through
her body. But there was no terror in it for her. Rather,
she felt almost as if she were standing back, watching
something happen on a stage.

She did know she was in mortal danger, that all of
them were.

The smoke coming in under the door was growing

thicker. Niki knew that they didn't have much time. She pressed her palm to the door. It was already hot.

Somehow, they had to find a way out. Maybe if they all worked together, they could break down the door, or bend back the grating.

She touched Terry's shoulder. "Terry!" she said. "We've got to do something!"

He just stared at her, his eyes full of pain and confusion. He couldn't hear anything she was saying, and he obviously couldn't think straight.

She tried Alex next, but like Terry he couldn't hear her. He turned away and went back to pulling on the grating with Murphy. "Has everyone lost their minds?" she said out loud. And realized that, in a way, they all had. Trisha and Angela were huddled together in a corner, sobbing, and Ricky was standing in front of the door, his eyes closed tightly, screaming.

None of her friends would be able to help her, Niki realized.

Maybe David would come soon with the police, but he'd been gone a long time. So many things could have happened to him that she knew she couldn't count on him now.

It was up to her.

Trying not to panic, and trying to ignore the growing clouds of smoke, she forced herself to think logically.

The door was too heavy to break through. She went over to the window and pushed in between Murphy and Alex. The grating was thick and immovable.

She stepped back and forced herself to take two or three deep breaths of the clear air coming in from the window. By now the smoke in the room had become thick as fog, and her friends were completely lost in their hysteria.

Justine had planned her revenge well.

If only there were another way out. If only there were a skylight, or a heating vent, or— Her eyes fell on a handle set in the wall. A small spark of hope jumped within her. It might be just a cupboard. But maybe . . .

She opened the small door and almost cried with relief.

It was part of the old dumbwaiter system that Justine had talked about. The dumbwaiter basket appeared to be much too small to hold a person, but Niki was slender, and besides, Justine had said that was how she'd gotten her into the basement.

With a sinking feeling Niki realized she wouldn't be able to lower the basket herself. It was designed to be lowered manually by someone pulling on a rope attached to a pulley. She would have to find help. But could she break through to any of her friends?

Terry was still sitting with his hands pressed tightly over his ears. She shook him, roughly. When he turned at her, she shouted as loud as she could. "Terry! You've got to help me!" He continued to stare at her blankly.

"Terry!" she called again. "Please! It's up to us!"

She searched his face, willing him to understand. Terry blinked and then suddenly his eyes cleared. He looked at her with understanding.

"Funny Face," he said.

The tape was much too loud for him to hear her. She pulled on his arm and led him over to the dumbwaiter. She pointed to herself, then to the basket, and pantomimed pulling on a rope. By now Alex had come over, too, and both boys were staring at her as if she had lost her mind.

"You can't!" Terry said. "It's too dangerous!"

Niki read his lips easily, but shrugged off his warning. She pointed to the dining-room door, where smoke was pouring in thicker and thicker.

"She's right!" Alex shouted. "It's our only chance!"

Reluctantly Terry nodded his agreement.

Good, Niki thought with relief. But would it work?

Together, Alex and Terry boosted her up to the entrance to the dumbwaiter. She took a deep breath and crawled into the basket. It was a tight fit, but by keeping her knees tucked up under her chin she was able to sit almost comfortably.

"Ready!" she shouted, her heart pounding furiously.

Alex began to operate the pulley. She could feel the ancient mechanism creaking and groaning under her weight. Would it hold her?

Suddenly the dumbwaiter basket caught on something. Looking up, she could see Alex and Terry pulling on the ropes, trying to free it.

It wouldn't budge.

The air in the shaft was hot and smelled of smoke. The fire was spreading quickly. If the basket didn't begin moving soon she would smother there inside the walls of the old house.

Knowing it was risky, she began to rock back and forth. She knew that it would either free her or cause the basket to fall the rest of the way to the basement.

With a sudden, sickening lurch, the basket dropped several inches.

Niki felt as if her heart had stopped, then she relaxed as the basket resumed its steady progress downward. At the bottom she pushed hard on the inside of the cupboard door and scrambled out.

The air was much cleaner there, and for a moment she just breathed. Then she switched on her flashlight and shone it around the dark, musty room.

The basement was shaped irregularly, and contained what seemed to be dozens of nooks and cupboards. How had Terry ever found her down there?

At last the flashlight showed the basement stairs, and she quickly ran up them, only to find that the door was scorching hot. If she opened it, she'd be incinerated.

There had to be another way out. There had to be!

Again she shone the flashlight around. Something dark and furry skittered off to one side, and Niki jumped. At last she saw the outlines of a window, and rushed over to it. Her heart sank in dismay.

It was boarded up.

Niki wanted to cry. After everything that had happened, to be trapped there, to die there . . .

Stop it! she told herself. Don't give up now.

Her friends were all depending on her. Terry was depending on her. Somehow, she had to find a way out.

She propped the flashlight so it shone on the boards over the window and began pulling at them, her fingernails all breaking. Finally one of the boards began to work loose, and she could see the dark shape of an overgrown bush outside.

She pulled harder and harder. At last the board came free.

The space wasn't quite big enough for her to escape

through, but if she could get one or two more boards loose, she might be able to wriggle out and go for help.

She began pulling on the next board, trying not to think about how long it was taking.

She had nearly pulled it free when she felt a hand squeeze her ankle.

chapter
21

Niki screamed and jumped away from the window. As she did, she tripped over something soft and went sprawling on the floor.

It's Justine, she thought.

Justine has found me and will kill me right now, right here.

But she won't do it without a fight.

Niki twisted and tried to pull away from the hand that held her.

But then, in the dim light from the flashlight, she saw that it wasn't Justine at all. It was Justine's uncle Philip. The hand that gripped her ankle was securely tied with rope to the other hand, and his ankles were tightly bound together. A large stain of dried blood showed on his white-and-blue polka-dot shirt.

Niki was so surprised that at first she didn't realize Philip was speaking to her. She squinted in the dim light and peered closely to see what he was saying.

"Help me," he said, his sad clown's face distorted by the urgency of his words. "Please, please, you've got to help!"

"I will," said Niki then. Philip stopped talking in surprise. "But you've got to help me too," she added. "Me and my friends."

She began to untie Philip's hands and feet, explaining as she did what Justine had done. When she told him about the fire, Philip's eyes widened in horror. "I thought I smelled smoke," he said. "I never dreamed that even she . . ."

Niki finished untying him. "Come on!" she said. "We've got to hurry!"

Philip scrambled to his feet and ran to a chest, returning with a thick crowbar. For such a frail-looking man he was surprisingly strong.

He pried the remaining boards off the window in only a few seconds. Then he lifted Niki onto the windowsill and scrambled after her.

Once outside, Niki greedily gulped in the fresh air.

But there was no time to waste. Niki and Philip ran around to the front of the house. Inside the windows they could see the glow of the fire. The other teens were all pressed against the window grate, struggling to breathe.

Philip pried at the grating with his crowbar.

No. No, it won't budge, thought Niki, the panic rising to her throat.

No. No.

Keep trying.

Yes!

At last Philip pulled off the grating.

Choking and gasping, the kids began to climb out,

their eyes red and streaming from the thick, acrid smoke.

Alex and Terry had helped the others out and were the last to emerge. An instant after they left, the door to the dining room burst into flames.

Niki and Philip led the choking, shocked kids out to the safety of the front yard, far from the house that was now in flames from the basement to the attic.

Once they had reached safety, Terry found Niki and hugged her tight, kissing her face and hair. "Funny Face," he said over and over, "Funny Face." Niki scarcely was able to believe he was all right. His face was streaked with soot and his eyebrows were slightly singed.

It had been close.

Very close.

Niki and Terry just stood there with their arms around each other, watching the burning house send up bright orange sparks into the sky.

To the east, faint streaks of light began to appear. Part of the roof suddenly caved in, sending a huge shower of sparks all over the lawn. Everyone moved back to the very edge of the yard. An instant later David stumbled out of the Fear Street woods.

"So I guess Marty and Bobby were too drunk to know what they were doing," David was explaining. "When I finally woke up, I was in a storage shed at the corner of the cemetery. I went over to the nearest house and called the police."

David had a huge bruise on his forehead and patches of dried blood on his cheeks, but he seemed to be all right.

In fact, everyone was. Everyone but Les.

Trisha and Ricky both were sitting and watching the fire almost as if nothing had happened to them. Murphy and Angela were sitting in the tall grass, ignoring how wet it was, comforting each other.

Alex was standing off by himself, a sad look on his face, the beautiful silver costume ripped and streaked with soot.

Terry couldn't believe it. How could so much happen in so short a time? He had a feeling that everything that had happened in that house that night had changed all of them—forever.

The faint wail of a siren began to sound in the distance.

Philip stood in front of the group of them, and Terry was surprised to see there were tears in his eyes. "I'm so terribly, terribly sorry," he told them. "I never meant anything like this to happen. You must believe me."

"What do you mean?" said Alex angrily. "We were almost killed in there!"

"All I wanted," said Philip, "was to frighten you. Nothing more."

Terry thought he was beginning to understand, and the knowledge enraged him. "Are you saying this was your idea all along?" he demanded.

"Yes," Philip said in a shamed voice. "You see, Justine's father was my older brother. He was the closest person to me in the world. After he died I vowed to raise Justine so he'd be proud of her. But I could never get over his death, and I guess through the years I must have communicated my bitterness to Justine. I see now I should have taught her forgiveness and love. Instead I taught her hatred and—the desire for revenge."

"Then you planned this all these years?" said Trisha, sounding horrified.

"No, not at all!" said Philip. He stopped and wiped his hand over his face. "Last year I became ill and decided to spend my last days in my brother's old home. I told everyone I was a distant cousin so they would leave me alone. But when Justine found out I was here, she left her boyfriend and career and moved in with me. She convinced me that I could never die in peace until I'd avenged my brother's death."

Terry stared at Philip in horror. Everything he was saying sounded like someone's nightmare—yet it was all true.

"You know the rest," Philip went on. "Justine enrolled in high school while I researched the original party and traced the sons and daughters of the teenagers involved in the accident. Then we sent the invitations."

"How could you do it?" Alex asked. "How? None of us ever did a thing to you!"

"I know it," said Philip. "And perhaps I *was* a little crazy to have carried a grudge for so long. But you must believe me! I never intended any real harm to come to you. I only wanted you to know terror, to know suffering for a while."

"But Justine took your plan one step too far, didn't she?" said Niki. In contrast to Alex, Niki's face and voice showed nothing but sympathy.

"I didn't realize how obsessed she had become," Philip said, nodding in agreement. "Until I found— found the body of your friend Les. I knew Justine had done it, and I knew I must stop her. I hid his body on the roof so no one would find it, and then I confronted my niece with what she had done. I told her we must stop the party at once. I told her I was going to call the police. But she—she—" He stopped speaking and began to sob.

"She attacked you," said Niki. "I know. She did it to me too."

"I never expected her to—to act against me," said Philip. "She stunned me with a blow to the head, and then she must have dragged me down to the basement and tied me up."

"Are you trying to tell us that Justine did all of this herself—killed Les, knocked you out—" Alex was plainly disbelieving.

"You must understand," said Philip, "that Justine is very strong. I think she worked on building up her strength so she would be capable of anything. I believe she always knew she would do something like this."

"How dare you?!"

Everyone turned at the sound of Justine's voice. She was standing at the edge of the garden, her lovely face almost unrecognizable beneath the madness and rage.

"Justine!" Philip cried. In spite of everything he had told them, Terry could see how much he still loved his niece.

"You have betrayed me!" Justine shouted at him. "Even worse, you've betrayed my parents! I should have killed you when I had the chance!"

"No!" cried Philip, sinking to his knees. "Don't say that!"

"I should have known you were too weak to do what had to be done!" she said. "No one was ever as strong

143

as I was. I planned the perfect revenge! And it would have succeeded—it nearly did succeed—" She glared at all of them with pure hatred.

Terry looked away. Niki gripped his hand more tightly.

We're safe now, he told himself. She can't hurt us anymore.

But he jumped in fright, as did everyone else, when Justine suddenly ran directly at them, her green eyes blank with madness.

Just before she reached them, she suddenly veered to the left, and then, moving faster than seemed possible, ran up the front steps and onto the burning porch.

chapter
22

"N_o!"

A single anguished wail from Philip split the air.

Terry froze when Justine had swerved and headed back to the burning house. But as soon as she reached the steps, he began running too, almost without realizing he was doing it.

Running after her.

Running toward the heat and the flames.

From the corner of his eye he sensed motion, and just as he reached the steps he saw that Alex, too, was running after Justine, just behind him.

Without slowing down, Terry ran up the steps and onto the blazing porch.

Justine was standing just at the entrance to the house, swaying slightly, her clothes beginning to burn. She turned around, and when she saw Alex and Terry her eyes widened and she started into the house, which had become an inferno of flame.

"Grab her!" Alex shouted.

Terry reached out and grabbed for Justine. He got her arm and pulled with all his strength. But with the strength of the insane, she lunged in the opposite direction, pulling him into the house after her.

Both of them tumbled onto the burning floor.

Terry screamed as he saw the flames, spreading to within inches of where he lay.

The next thing he knew, someone had grabbed him, and he was rolling out of the house, down the steps, and into the mud. Someone rolled him over and over, the cool mud soothing the heat.

He sat up, dazed, to see Alex standing over Justine, beating out her flaming clothes with his silver jacket.

Justine was sobbing now, not in insanity, but in defeat, and pain.

Alex came over and bent over Terry, his pale face frightened and drawn.

"Hey, man," he said. "You all right?"

Terry nodded. "You saved my life, Alex. Thanks."

"You tried to save all our lives," Alex said, putting a hand on Terry's shoulder. "I guess we were just too stubborn to listen."

For a moment the two boys just stared at each other, and Terry saw something he had never expected to see again—the look of friendship and respect. He hoped that his face showed the same things.

A moment later the yard filled with the flashing lights and wailing sirens of emergency vehicles. While the firemen began to battle the blaze, medical personnel examined Terry and Alex for burns.

Niki stood close beside Terry, holding on to his arm as if she would never let go. "What do you think will happen to Justine?" she said.

"She will get the help she needs," said Philip sadly. "I should have seen that she had it long ago."

They watched as Justine was strapped onto a hospital gurney.

A few minutes later the police ambulance pulled out of the yard, its siren wailing.

Overhead a shower of sparks erupted, illuminating the ruined skeleton of the Cameron mansion.

Behind the black smoke, the red morning sun made its first appearance.

"Hey—we made it all night. It's morning!" Ricky cried. "It isn't Halloween anymore!"

"I don't know about that," said Niki, holding on to Terry's arm as they began to walk away. "It's always Halloween on Fear Street."

About the Author

R.L. Stine invented the teen horror genre with Fear Street, the bestselling teen horror series of all time. He also changed the face of children's publishing with the mega-successful Goosebumps series, which *Guinness World Records* cites as the Best-Selling Children's Book Series ever, and went on to become a worldwide multimedia phenomenon. The first two books in his new series Mostly Ghostly, *Who Let the Ghosts Out?* and *Have You Met My Ghoulfriend?*, are *New York Times* bestsellers. He's thrilled to be writing for teens again in the brand-new Fear Street Nights books.

R.L. Stine has received numerous awards of recognition, including several Nickelodeon Kids' Choice Awards and Disney Adventures Kids' Choice Awards, and he has been selected by kids as one of their favorite authors in the National Education Association Read Across America. He lives in New York City with his wife, Jane, and their dog, Nadine.

DEAR READERS,

WELCOME TO **FEAR STREET**—WHERE YOUR WORST NIGHTMARES LIVE! IT'S A TERRIFYING PLACE FOR SHADYSIDE HIGH STUDENTS—AND FOR **YOU!**

DID YOU KNOW THAT THE SUN NEVER SHINES ON THE OLD MANSIONS OF FEAR STREET? NO BIRDS CHIRP IN THE FEAR STREET WOODS. AND AT NIGHT, EERIE MOANS AND HOWLS RING THROUGH THE TANGLED TREES.

I'VE WRITTEN NEARLY A HUNDRED FEAR STREET NOVELS, AND I AM THRILLED THAT MILLIONS OF READERS HAVE ENJOYED ALL THE FRIGHTS AND CHILLS IN THE BOOKS. WHEREVER I GO, KIDS ASK ME WHEN I'M GOING TO WRITE A NEW FEAR STREET TRILOGY.

WELL, NOW I HAVE SOME EXCITING NEWS. I HAVE WRITTEN A BRAND-NEW FEAR STREET TRILOGY. THE THREE NEW BOOKS ARE CALLED **FEAR STREET NIGHTS**. THE SAGA OF SIMON AND ANGELICA FEAR AND THE UNSPEAKABLE EVIL THEY CAST OVER THE TEENAGERS OF SHADYSIDE WILL CONTINUE IN THESE NEW BOOKS. YES, SIMON AND ANGELICA FEAR ARE BACK TO BRING TERROR TO THE TEENS OF SHADYSIDE.

FEAR STREET NIGHTS IS AVAILABLE NOW. . . . DON'T MISS IT. I'M VERY EXCITED TO RETURN TO FEAR STREET—AND I HOPE YOU WILL BE THERE WITH ME FOR ALL THE GOOD, SCARY FUN!

RL Stine

feel the fear.

EAR STREET® NIGHTS

A brand-new Fear Street trilogy by the master of horror

R.L. STINE

In Stores Now

Simon Pulse
Published by Simon & Schuster
FEAR STREET is a registered trademark of Parachute Press, Inc.

CHERUB

a division of MI5

by Robert Muchamore

The kid playing GameBoy on the steps. That skater punk who cut you off. The girl reading a book at the front of the bus.

You may walk right by. You don't even notice them. But they're all secret agents. CHERUB employs more than two hundred fifty agents, all under the age of seventeen.

They hack into computers.
They spy on terrorists.
And they're always watching.
Because no one suspects them.

quarantine eyes

1 2 3 4 5 6 7 8 9 10

How many stars?

Barney??

life has never felt this beautiful

IN LOVE

the best Halloween time of the year!